EVERY
YOU, ME
EVERY

ALSO BY DAVID LEVITHAN

Boy Meets Boy
The Realm of Possibility
Are We There Yet?
Wide Awake
How They Met, and Other Stories
Love Is the Higher Law

WITH RACHEL COHN

Nick & Norah's Infinite Playlist
Naomi and Ely's No Kiss List
Dash & Lily's Book of Dares

EVERY YOU, EVERY ME

by david levithan

photographs by jonathan farmer

EMBER

 Published in the United States by Ember, an imprint of Random House Children's Books, a division of Random House, Inc., New York.
Originally published in hardcover in the United States by Alfred A. Knopf, an imprint of Random House Children's Books, New York, in 2011.

Ember and the E colophon are registered trademarks of Random House, Inc.

Visit us on the Web! randomhouse.com/teens

Educators and librarians, for a variety of teaching tools, visit us at randomhouse.com/teachers

The Library of Congress has cataloged the hardcover edition of this work as follows:
Levithan, David.
Every you, every me / by David Levithan ; photographs by Jonathan Farmer.
p. cm.
Summary: Evan is haunted by the loss of his best friend, but when mysterious photographs start appearing, he begins to fall apart as he starts to wonder if she has returned, seeking vengeance.
ISBN 978-0-375-86098-0 (trade) — ISBN 978-0-375-96098-7 (lib. bdg.) —
ISBN 978-0-375-89621-7 (ebook)
[1. Mental illness—Fiction. 2. Emotional problems—Fiction.
3. Interpersonal relations—Fiction. 4. Friendship—Fiction. 5. High schools—Fiction.
6. Schools—Fiction.] I. Farmer, Jonathan, ill. II. Title.
PZ7.L5798Ev 2011
[Fic]—dc22
2010048723

ISBN 978-0-375-85451-4 (pbk.)

RL: 6.9

Printed in the United States of America

10 9 8 7 6 5 4 3 2

First Ember Edition 2012

To Jake Hamilton
(for living photographically)
—DL

To Mom and Dad
—JF

1

It was your birthday. The first one after you ~~left vanished~~ were gone.

When I woke up, I ~~dreamed~~ thought about other birthdays. Ones where we'd been together.

Like two years ago. Freshman year. ~~When I had you all to myself.~~ I asked you what you wanted and you said roses, and then you said, "But not the flowers." So I spent weeks gathering presents: a polished piece of rose quartz, White Rose tea, a ceramic tile I'd bought at the White House in fourth grade featuring the Rose Garden. A novel called *Rose Sees Red*, a biography of Gypsy Rose Lee, a mix of songs by bands called Blue Roses, the Stone Roses, White Rose Movement. Then I rigged your locker with pulleys, so when you opened it, all the objects *rose*. I'm not sure you got that part, not until I told you. But you were so happy then. ~~This was before happiness became so complicated. This was when you could ask me for something, I could give it to you, and the world would be right.~~

And then there was last year. ~~You went out with Jack at night, but I at least had you for the afternoon.~~ I asked you what you wanted and you said you didn't want anything. And I told you I wasn't planning on giving you anything; I was planning on giving you something. That whole week, we started to divide things into those two categories: *anything* or *something*. A piece of jewelry bought at a department store: *anything*. A piece of jewelry made by hand: *something*. A dollar: *anything*. A sand dollar: *something*. A gift certificate: *anything*. An IOU for two hours of starwatching: *something*. A drunk kiss at a party: *anything*. A sober kiss alone in a park: *something*. We ended up spending the afternoon walking around, pointing at things and labeling them *anything* or *something*. ~~Should I have paid closer attention? Written them down? No, it was a good day. Wasn't it?~~ At the end, you pointed to me and said *something*. And I pointed back and said *something*. ~~I held on to that.~~

Now it was a year later. I wished you a happy birthday. ~~That word again. *Happy*. It's a curse. The pursuit of happiness makes us deeply unhappy. It's a trap.~~

Before anything else happened, there was me in bed, thinking of ~~who~~ you ~~used to be~~.

I don't want you to think I forgot.

1A

I see too many things at once. I notice shadows. Think about them. And while I do that, I miss other things. Important things. I can't stop looking, even when I ~~want to~~ have to stop. I get lost in ifs. They are always there ~~*if if if if*~~ and I should only be able to tune in to them if I'm on the right frequency. But that's the thing about me: The frequencies don't divide.

~~That day was your birthday in my head, but it wasn't really your birthday anywhere else.~~ I wanted to tell people at school that it was your birthday ~~but I didn't want to get their reaction when I brought it up~~. I started to think it was like a surprise party, only they weren't telling either of us. They were going to surprise both of us. ~~I didn't have this thought for long. It was really just there for a moment.~~ I pretended like it was a normal day ~~without you there~~. And like all other normal days, I made it through to the other end. ~~It can be done, you see.~~

There are things you decide ~~and there are decisions you don't even know you are making~~. That afternoon, I decided to cut through the woods on my way home. ~~As I headed that way, I looked at the ground, not the branches or the sky. If I'd stopped to~~

~~talk to someone after school instead of heading straight home—if I'd had someone to talk to—maybe someone else would have gotten there first. I didn't decide to see the envelope.~~ I saw the envelope sitting there on the ground. ~~I should have left it alone. I should have been left alone. I was alone.~~ I stopped and picked it up. From the weight, I knew there was something inside. I decided to open it.

~~I wasn't thinking of you.~~

It was so small. I had to focus. I couldn't focus without telling myself to focus. ~~*The eyes take in the colors and the shapes. The images go to the brain for translation.*~~ First I saw the trees, then the sky. It didn't look familiar. ~~*The brain cross-checks the translation against the memories it's stored.*~~ I fixed on the four bare trees, standing like orphaned table legs. I knew those trees—I looked away from the photo and there they were in real life, no more than twenty feet away from me. I walked over to the nearest tree, but that didn't tell me anything. I looked at the envelope, but it was completely blank. ~~No address, no name on the front. I looked.~~ I almost put it back. But the sky was getting gray, almost as gray as the sky in the photo. Leaving it on the ground didn't seem right. It was going to rain.

I saw the other trees. I held the photo up against real life, figured out my place in it. But there was something I was missing. ~~Or maybe there was something extra. I was here. I was not in the photograph. Therefore the photograph was then, and I was now.~~ Where was the photo taken from?

I turned around and saw my school. Its windows. Watching me.

Revealing nothing.

~~*Anything? Something?*~~

I put the photograph back in the envelope. ~~I didn't put the envelope back on the ground.~~ I kept it. And I might have forgotten about it. I might have just thrown it out, or let it stay in my backpack until it became crumpled and torn and wrecked on the bottom with all the pieces of unchewed gum slipped loose from their wrappers. I might have just shown it to Jack or someone else the next day at school. ~~In another time, I would have shown it to you first.~~ We would have shrugged and moved on to the next thing. It would have been a short, short story.

Random, we would have said.

Random.

Meaning:

Completely without a pattern.

or

Completely without a *recognizable* pattern.

~~Meaning:~~

~~Either the event is outside any pattern.~~

~~or~~

~~We are unable to comprehend the pattern.~~

I folded the envelope in half, careful that the photo wasn't caught in the crease.

(I try to be a careful person. Most of the time my carelessness is completely unintentional.)

I looked around one more time, stood in the center of the bare trees, at the exact center.

Then I headed home and I lost focus and the barrage in my head started again.

~~*You will never be happy again. Why do you even think about it?*~~

Five minutes after I picked up the photo, it rained.

~~*This pain is all that you have.*~~

I think:

If I'd been five minutes later, it would have been raining   if it had been five minutes later, I would have been dashing through the rain, not noticing   if I'd been five minutes later, the envelope and the photo would have been soaked, ruined.

I think:

If I'd been five minutes later, none of this would have happened.

I know:

It probably would have happened anyway. Just not like this.

1B

I woke up at two in the morning, feeling guilty that I hadn't asked you what you wanted this year.

2

The next morning I returned to the same spot. I didn't tell myself I was going to do it. I just walked there. It was still cloudy; the sun had risen, but I couldn't really see it. It was like the day had no hours. I only knew it was morning because I was so tired.

I hadn't really slept. ~~I never really sleep anymore.~~

I didn't expect there to be anything to find, so I was surprised when I saw the second envelope.

It wasn't in the same spot as the first one. This time it was in the exact center of the four bare trees. Like someone had drawn an X between them, and the envelope marked the crossing point. ~~The crosshairs.~~

The ground was still wet, and as I walked over it, my boots sank a little. Even though it was so close to school, nobody was around. It was too early for them. Everyone else was asleep. I was the morning watchman.

~~Only what could be safe with me? What could I protect? I hadn't been able to stop harm. I'd harmed.~~

I picked up the envelope and looked at it. Still no address, no clue. Sealed blankness.

~~I wanted more of your handwriting. After you were gone, I realized how little of it I had.~~

I ripped open the envelope and shook the photo out into my hand.

This time, it was a much bigger surprise.

It was a picture of me.

I was the photo.

2A

Nobody ever took my picture. They didn't want to. Or I wouldn't let them.

You were the only exception.

2B

I looked all around. Into the woods. At the school. Down the path. The full 360. ~~*"So it's all come full circle," you said.*~~ I didn't feel like I was being watched, but the possibility was there.

The only possibility that was gone was the possibility of randomness. Because it was me inside the envelope. Because the envelope was dry. Because it hadn't stopped raining until about an hour ago. Because that meant whoever had left it had come out at daybreak to do it. Maybe he or she knew I'd be here early. Maybe he or she knew me and what time I'd be here.

~~You would have known that. Jack would have known that.~~

It felt a little less like a mystery and more like a game. A trick. ~~A trap.~~

I put the photo in the envelope and the envelope in my pocket. I wondered why my name hadn't been written on it. What if someone else had found it?

The rest of the walk to school, my mind returned to zeros and ones. ~~This 001110101110 is 011101100110 a 10011101 language 111111000000.~~ Focused on nothing, open to everything—it's a state I fall into, where all my senses swap. My voice is blind, my hearing is mute, my sight is deaf. Art is science, mathematics is conversation, and music is something that bleeds. I am so far away that I'm inside myself. I barely notice colors unless I taste them. Not the yellows or the greens. I taste the deeper blues. The darker reds.

~~You see, I understand.~~

The school doors were still locked, so I sat on the patio in the back. It was just me and a collection of wet cigarette butts ~~one two three four five six countless~~, and I wondered if it would be possible to make a language out of their arrangement. Was it a pattern or was it chaos? I always thought that if I looked long enough, I could find the pattern. ~~010011000111000001111~~ And if I didn't look long enough, there would be chaos. ~~*At first, I could not understand the screaming.*~~

My thoughts always exist within a windstorm; they have to be strongly rooted in order to stay. So when Jack finally joined me, I had already forgotten about the photo. I thought of you and looked for you next to him, as if my mind suddenly believed it was two months ago. I saw that his hair was longer, that the peak in the front was a little higher, a little blonder than what I usually pictured when I pictured him. ~~*Remember when you were happy? Well, it's a lie.*~~ I felt like there was something I had to tell him. I noticed someone turning on the lights in the school library.

~~*Good morning, library.*~~

"How long have you been here?" he asked. He didn't look awake yet, like his synapses were still cloudy even though his body was going through the morning motions.

"Not long," I said, mostly because I had no idea how long it had been.

"What'd you do last night?"

~~I never do anything.~~ "Not much. You?"

"Nothing."

I never knew if Jack came to the patio this early because he knew I'd be there, or if he would've done it anyway. We were ~~best~~ friends ~~by default~~ but it was like our friendship was never fully awake, either. We were each closer to you than we were to each other. Your absence dulled us.

Jack took out a cigarette and asked, "You mind?"

He always asked, and I always said I didn't, even though I did. ~~*Why do you want to put more smoke inside of you?*~~

~~You said you hated his smoking, but you didn't really, not in the way that you hated other things, like life.~~

He lit up and took drags in between sips of coffee. My attention started to scatter into details, like the way his lip stuck for a second on the plastic coffee-cup lid or the weight of the ashes that fell from his cigarette. You think ashes float, but really they just gather together until there are enough of them to fall straight down. ~~That was something you would see. That was something you would say.~~

I remembered the photo in my pocket and took out the envelope.

"This yours?" I asked.

"What is it?"

"I found it. There's a picture inside."

Jack shook his head, exhaled some smoke. It matched the color of the sky, but I could still tell when it disappeared.

"Not mine," he said. "Where'd you find it?"

"Near the woods."

"What's in it?"

"I told you, a picture."

Jack took one last drag, then dropped the cigarette and stepped on it. He reached out his hand and I passed the envelope over to him. As he opened it, I could feel the smoke on his fingers painting itself onto the envelope. ~~*Taint.*~~ The cigarette on the ground was still burning.

"Hey, that's a good photo of you," he said. "Who took it?"

"I don't know. That's the point. I don't know." Then I told him the whole story about finding the first photograph, and how whoever took it must have taken one of me while I was finding the first one.

"Fascinating," Jack said, but it was clear from the sound of his voice that the fascination wouldn't last much longer than the cigarette had.

"So it wasn't you?" I asked.

"No," he said, still looking at the photo.

"Maybe it was Ariel?"

~~*Say her name.*~~

Now Jack looked up, a little bit tired of me.

"Ev, you know it couldn't have been Ariel."

~~He said your name.~~

"What if she's back?"

Jack returned the photo and lit another cigarette, this time not asking me if it was okay.

"Ev, she's not back."

"But what if . . ."

"It's not her."

"So some random stranger took my picture yesterday and left it for me this morning?"

"It wasn't yesterday."

"What?"

He leaned over and pointed to the photo, his cigarette jutting out from between his fingers, chimneying his hand.

"You weren't wearing that yesterday. And there wasn't that much sun yesterday. This is from another day."

I tried. I really tried to think of when someone might have taken my picture. Not posed. Not premeditated. Spontaneous.

But no.

~~You were the only exception.~~

"Freaky," Jack said. Then he looked away from me, at the other people who were on the patio with us. ~~Seeing us as two friends talking. Our morning routine. Everything routine.~~ They'd appeared without me noticing. My brain took them off mute. I heard their voices without making out the words.

Freaky. That was Jack's conclusion. And I knew it was pointless to talk to him about anything after he'd come to a conclusion.

Still, I had to ask.

"Have you heard from her?"

He shook his head.

"It's a good photo," he said. Then we went inside and split off into our own trajectories.

There were so many voices, so many people around me. I stood there on the side of the hallway and watched everyone pass—some traveling together, some meeting up, most entirely unaware of anything besides where they were going, each particle knowing its own destination without ever knowing the exact path. ~~Is this what you meant when you said you were splitting?~~ Every step, even the smallest movement, marking a different line. I started plotting out the variations of my own route—not just the ways I could go, but all the people I might step a little bit aside for, or slow down for, or speed up to see. I was starting to get lost in my own infinities, so I refocused on the faces, on the people I knew and the people I recognized and the people who seemed familiar and the people who were strangers even though we had this school in common. There were two thousand of us in this building, and one of them, I thought, was responsible for the photograph in my pocket. One of the two thousand was responsible for the envelopes and the mystery and my thoughts at that exact moment. One of them had done it.

~~Unless it was the girl who wasn't here.~~

2C

~~I'm lying, aren't I?~~

~~I never wanted you to take my picture. You did, but I never really wanted it.~~

~~We were at the pool. It had to be summer. I didn't want to take my shirt off. I never took my shirt off. But you said I was being ridiculous. That was your word. *Ridiculous*. Mostly friendly, but a little teasing. You asked me what I was ashamed of. Had I carved Molly Hughes's name on my chest? Were there unicorn tattoos I hadn't told you about? Was I wearing a man girdle? I wasn't really laughing, but I wasn't not laughing. You tugged at my shirt. I said fine and took it off. Felt the sun. Felt so pale. And you took out your camera. Said you had to capture this for posterity.~~

~~I felt like I was your accomplishment, when what I really wanted was to be your friend.~~

~~"You see," you said, "you have nothing to hide."~~

~~I didn't want you to see me with my shirt off. It was weird.~~

~~I never saw the picture. You might have deleted it.~~

~~I mean, I doubt you still have it.~~

~~Did the accomplishment mean anything in the end?~~

3

I went back to the spot after school, but there wasn't any new photo there. Same thing the next morning. Even though I knew two points didn't make a pattern, I was still disappointed to find nothing there. It couldn't just end. Not now.

3A

~~*You are leaving me messages, but I haven't gotten the message yet.*~~

3B

I took out my notebook. I ripped out a page. I wrote *WHO ARE YOU?* across the top and left the rest of it blank. I moved the second photograph into the first photograph's envelope, then stuck the note in the empty one. I left it there before meeting up with Jack on the patio.

When I ran back between second and third periods, the envelope was gone.

But there wasn't anything left in its place.

3C

I checked during lunch. I checked after school.

The spot was empty. Empty but not void. Void is when there is absolutely nothing there and the nothing is natural, a complete vacuum. But empty—with empty, you are aware of what's supposed to be there. Empty means something is missing.

Once again, a grayness was settling in. ~~My mood.~~ The light around me was changing its properties. ~~I tried to catch it dimming, but it was imperceptible.~~

I started walking home. The normal route.

I was trying to connect the words in my head when I saw it. Nailed to a telephone pole. Another envelope.

Not taped there. Not tacked up. Nailed. At my eye level. Precisely.

I wondered how long it had been there. I wondered why nobody else had seen it. I wondered if I'd passed by it on my way to school, missing it because I didn't look back.

But most of all I wondered what was inside.

For some reason, I was expecting an answer to the question I'd left behind: *Who are you?* I wanted the photographer to leave me a self-portrait.

Instead I got more trees. This time with a wall, curving into an arch at its top.

3D

3E

I figured I had to go back into the woods, directly from this spot. ~~I wouldn't find you there. I knew I wouldn't find you there.~~ It couldn't be a coincidence that the photographer had chosen this pole. ~~*Coincidence. Things coinciding.*~~ The tree line was to my right. I'd never ventured this way before ~~had I~~? but I imagined it would all be the same when I got inside. And by *imagined* I mean I really did imagine it—I sent a mental search party walking there even before I'd moved a step, picturing it like it existed. Then, from that single section of wall, that single set of stones, I built an entire castle. I imagined a fortress waiting in the middle of the forest—not with a sleeping beauty inside, but haunted by a sleeping beauty's ghost. The body would have decayed to dust, showing that all beauty is temporary, except perhaps in stories. My mind was getting away from reality again, and I reluctantly drew it back in. ~~There is no getting away from reality. Well, only one way.~~ I knew there were no castles in this small patch of suburban thicket. You, Jack, and I would have found them by now. We would have known.

We had been kids here once.

"Ariel!" I called out now like I'd called out then. When you'd been hiding. When I'd seeked.

~~Remember?~~

~~You never answered. Not with words. Sometimes you'd simply look over from wherever you were, and that small movement would help me find you. Other times you'd wait. And if it grew dark and I hadn't found you, I knew to go to your backyard steps. If you weren't already waiting for me there, I waited for you. You always returned. Until you and Jack started up. For a time, I still waited for you, even though I knew you were somewhere together, maybe inside. Then I stopped waiting.~~

It was too dim now. I was unfamiliar with this nonpath. I walked through the woods, lost, making my own wrongheaded trail. Then I got to a spot. Not the spot I was looking for, but another spot—a spot I remembered. You and I had been here, on this kind of a day, with the clouds venturing too close to the ground, too deep into my thoughts. We came into the woods because nobody else did. ~~When you weren't with Jack, you were mine again.~~ Last year. It must have been late last year. We'd escaped into the trees to hold hands and talk. This wasn't unusual for us to do, ~~I loved it so much~~ and I wouldn't have remembered this time as different from any of the others if it hadn't been for what you'd said.

~~I don't want to remember this. But I have no more control over my memories than I do over the past.~~

"If I ever ask you to get me a gun," you said, "could you?"

At first I'd thought it was a joke. I asked you what kind of gun.

~~Remember?~~

"The shooting kind," you answered. "A real gun."

That's when I knew it wasn't a game or a joke. It was a test. ~~A trap.~~

"What are you talking about?" I said.

And you repeated, "If I ever ask you to get me a gun, could you?"

"A gun?"

"Yes, a gun."

Nobody in my house owned a gun. Nobody in my life.

I told you this.

"But would you go out and find one for me? If I told you I really needed one."

~~I'd wanted to say *You're crazy*, but already those were dangerous words.~~

You were facing me, but your expression was all zeros. Your hand was resting on the bark of a tree, and that's what my eye fixed on. I wondered why we call a tree's skin *bark* instead of just *skin*. I wondered if it was because ours is so weak in comparison.

"Evan," you said, bringing me back.

"I couldn't get you a gun," I told you.

"But if you could, would you?"

"Why are you asking me this?"

~~I thought I could contain it. I thought I could prevent it.~~

You moved your hand from the tree. Walked over to me and nestled in. I thought that was it. I thought we were moving on.

But then you said it, in a matter-of-fact voice.

"If I ever ask you to get me a gun, don't. Whatever I say,

don't." Looking right into my eyes. "Listen to me, Evan. If I ever ask for that, go get help. If I ever ask for that, you're going to have to save me."

~~Plus/minus~~
~~Positive/negative~~
~~1/0~~
~~I can/I can't~~
~~I will/I won't~~
~~You are/you aren't~~
~~I said/I thought~~
~~I said "I will"/I thought *I can't*~~
~~I thought *I can*/I said "You won't"~~

There's no way to release yourself from a memory. It ends when it wants to end, whether it's in a flash or long after you've begged it to stop. What was the next line? What did I say to you then? I probably changed the subject, and the new subject wasn't worth remembering. So I was back in the present, back in the woods, photograph in hand. I heard cars in the distance. I let myself be hit by branches. I did not walk aimlessly—I had an aim—but I walked mindlessly. I heard the tops of the trees being shaken by wind. I looked for walls. I stopped calling your name.

It was unfair, I thought—the photograph had made the leaves white. I was looking for things that weren't as they were.

Then I realized I could be walking on top of what I was looking for.

And I thought, *Of course*.

3F

There was a place where the woods dropped. There was a path. And a bridge. A small bridge. A small stone bridge.

I ran as if someone was waiting for me. As if I was late.

~~*"Listen to me, Evan. If I ever ask for that, go get help. If I ever ask for that, you're going to have to save me."*~~

~~*I tried I tried I tried I*~~

It was about ten minutes farther in. This strange stone bridge, patching the gap between two cliffs. A memento of some earlier settlers, who might have had uses for the forest that were obscure to us now.

~~*It was your mind. What could I do?*~~

Focus, I thought. *Focus*.

I skidded down the dirt edge of one of the cliffs. I felt like I was bruising myself, but I didn't mind. I saw the arch but couldn't see if anything was in it. Anyone. ~~I wanted you to be waiting with your camera. I wanted to be blinded by a flash, hear a laugh behind it.~~

Nothing stirred as I approached. The bridge had been out of use so long that the trees and the shrubs had begun to grow underneath it. ~~Abandoned.~~ I stepped through the undergrowth and looked through to the other side.

"Hello?" I called.

I had gotten so used to being alone, but never entirely used to it. ~~Never used to it enough to stop wanting the alternative.~~

I jabbed my shoulder against the wall, made another bruise. The stones curved right over my head. They were cold, colder than the air.

I started to find patterns in the way the stones were stacked, and that's when I saw it. Shoved into the bridge like a message that had been left for the rocks.

The next envelope.

As I reached up, I flashed into a fit of frequencies—all of them playing at once. ~~Your voice, saying you would never forgive me.~~ The first envelope sitting on the ground, my hand reaching down for it. My mother telling me not to touch things as we walked through a museum. Or maybe it was someone's house. The curve of the stone next to the crack. And the crack itself—the shape of it, how it grabbed hold of the envelope. Hunger and sounds and my shirt pulling up as I reached, exposing the skin. ~~The bark.~~ I thought about the castle this was supposed to be, and wasn't. ~~Your prison.~~ Jack's cigarette. The fire that receded to the tip of his mouth and the smoke that expanded into the air. Two infinities: the one that stretches to the beginning but never touches—when you halve and halve and halve and halve, infinitely—and then the one that spreads out into the endless, endless future, the endless, endless distance. The set of infinities that is itself infinite. ~~*How do we go on? When so much happens to us, how do we*~~

~~*go on?*~~ I took the envelope in my hand. I was already picturing myself opening it. I was already ahead of myself. But I had to stop that image—I had to stop that prediction—because I had no idea what was going to be inside.

Like every fool before me, I reached.

4

4A

~~It was your mind. The way you were wired. That was the only thing all the theories had in common. You were manic. You were depressive. You were schizophrenic. You were on drugs. You were on the wrong medication. You needed medication. You heard voices. You'd lost the will to speak. Anxiety. Disorder. Nobody knew for sure, at least nobody who was saying anything. After you left, all that remained were guesses. I would go over everything. Every detail. Every panic. Every sigh. But they never added up to anything but you. I only saw the person. I couldn't see the wiring. I couldn't fix the wiring.~~

~~I tried I tried~~ I

4B

At first I needed daylight to see it—or any light—because it was too dark to make out anything in the tunnel. I needed the articulation of light—or at least I thought that would be enough. But then when I was outside again, the image still wasn't clear to me. We were still in the woods, yes. And there was a figure. But who? What? It could be Bigfoot staring at me.

I needed magnification. Because if I kept on staring, the photograph would become the stories I made for it, and I'd have no way to get back to the truth.

~~*"You're not making this up," your mother said. "Are you?"*~~

I ~~ran~~ went home and attacked the drawers. I needed a magnifying glass. I had no idea why we would have one, but it seemed like the kind of thing every house would have. Hammer, egg timer, magnifying glass. I was opening drawers I hadn't opened in years. In my top desk drawer I found stamps that were now devalued, ink pads that had dried up, a rubber zoo of pencil-top erasers shaped like cartoon characters. It was like my childhood had fallen overboard from my life and had washed up here, in secret. But no magnifying glass.

~~But I still have your sunglasses. You left them at my house. I guess that means they're mine now. I'd give them back if I could. I keep them on my desk. I can't bring myself to put them away. They don't look good on me. I remembered one time I tried and you laughed and said that there wasn't a pair of sunglasses in the world that didn't make me in some way look like a douche. You said I had honest eyes, and that I shouldn't try to hide them.~~

I checked the kitchen drawer that held all of the things that didn't belong in any of the other kitchen drawers—the pot holders, the scissors, the glue stick. Nothing. I checked my dad's desk drawer, with its language of paper clips and binder clips. Nothing. I checked in my mother's desk drawer—just old business cards and notes and a few photographs of me from when I was younger, much younger, extremely young. ~~*Was I always like this?*~~

And then my mind started getting so angry at itself. ~~*I know I suck. I know I'm stupid. Stop telling me. I know.*~~ Because the answer had been here all along.

I loaded up our computer. Turned on the scanner. Placed the photo on top of the glass operating table. Pressed a few buttons. Turned away from the light.

The scanner translated the photo into pixels. Then it translated the pixels into zeros and ones. Then it translated the zeros and ones into pixels again, which in turn were assembled into an image on the screen.

I clicked zoom.

And again.

And again.

200 percent.

And again.

And again. And again. I kept clicking until the photograph was demolished, until it was no more than a mosaic of gray tiles, adding up to nothing. *Nothing*. ~~Because wasn't that how I felt that day? If you zoom close—if you really get close to someone, if you really get close to yourself—then you lose the other person, you lose yourself entirely. You get so close you can't see anything anymore. Your mind becomes all these abstract fragments. English becomes math.~~

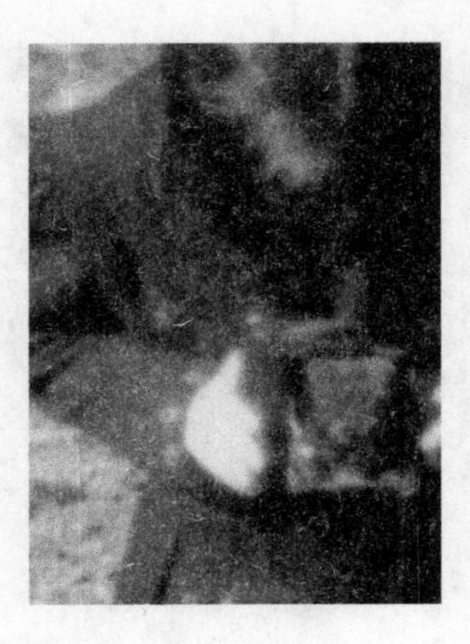

I zoomed until all that was left was squares. Sixteen. Then six. Then four.

The computer stopped me at four.

These four squares told me the truth. I no longer recognized what part of the photo they came from. They could be leaves.

They could be part of my hair. My skin. The antique camera in my hand. The dirt. All I knew was which day they came from. Unmistakably.

Somebody else had been there that day.

~~Somebody had seen us.~~

4C

I knew I should have called Jack, should have told him . . . but I didn't. ~~Not yet. I was afraid of him thinking that I was crazy, too.~~ I wasn't sure ~~what he'd do if he saw me drowning. I wasn't sure he'd save me unless he was also saving himself.~~ what he'd say.

5

I walked past your house later that night. My mind was still full of pixels, so I tried to pixelate everything I was seeing. Turn the lamps into white squares, the road into gray. Your house, though, defied this. ~~I know it's not your house now but it's still your house.~~ It insisted on being noticed on its own terms. *You did this to me*, it said. Not in a voice ~~I wasn't hearing voices (yet)~~ but in the way it sat there in the night. There was something missing from it, and I was the cause, I was the one who knew. There were lights on, but I couldn't tell if that meant anyone was home. You told me how your parents always left lights on when they went away, set on timers to mimic bedtime. I loved it when we reset them, even when your parents were around. Under our control, the lights in the house would go on for three minutes—from 3:01 a.m. to 3:04 a.m.—shining through the neighborhood, casting shadows. Your parents were always asleep. They never knew. ~~They always slept well, until Jack and I woke them up.~~

I liked your parents. I always thought that when the story was told, they would see me as the hero. But instead I became the bearer of their sorrows. ~~*"You're not making this up, are you?"*~~ I showed up, gave them the burden, and left. I missed the burden now. Even if I couldn't have handled it, I wished the heroic thing would have been to keep ~~you~~ it for myself.

It could not have been your parents in the woods that day. Neither of them could have taken the photograph. ~~Nobody who really knew you could have. They would have tried to stop it. They would have intervened.~~

They would not have stood and watched and taken pictures.

5A

~~Do they sleep? I want to know . . . am I the only one who doesn't sleep?~~

5B

I knew you were at the center of it.

This should not have surprised me, since you had always been at the center of things. Nobody would have put you anywhere else. Especially me.

Even now, you refused to be ~~pixelated, forgotten, silenced,~~ erased. Not that I wanted to erase you. The opposite. I wanted the opposite.

5C

Ours wasn't the kind of friendship where I knew the exact day it started. I only knew the exact day it became essential.

I have always been aware of how I break.
I know what kind of situations will break me.
I know what kind of people will do it.
I know how much it will hurt.

That day in sixth grade, ~~remember~~? I broke because the humiliations and doubts and anger gained critical mass. I failed a history test because I'd forgotten about it; I had been studying hard all year, and with one bad grade I undid it all. Then I had to run an extra two laps in gym because I was too ~~"lazy"~~ slow, and I didn't think I was going to make it, and I was going to have to stop or die of a lung attack before I finished. The other kids loved that. And then, at lunch, I tried to sit with Tara Jenkins and she told me there was no room, even though there was. The weight of it was too much. I felt myself breaking as I went outside to recess. I found a quiet piece of pavement and started rubbing my hand over it. Catching the gravel in my skin until I was bleeding, until my palm was open and raw.

Then you found me. Later, you'd tell me that you'd seen what Tara had done and had followed me out to see if I was okay. ~~I was never sure if that was true. I thought it was possible you happened to see what I was doing and were morbidly intrigued.~~ You came over to me and didn't tell me I was gross and didn't ask me what I was doing. Instead you said, "Stop that." And I did.

I said I hated life. You said you hated life. We decided to hate it together.

~~We didn't know anything.~~

Without you I wouldn't have been able to contain the hate. I would have used it against myself. You're the one who helped me control it. My mind spun out to other things.

But it always came back to you.

5D

They said you weren't coming back.
I didn't believe them.
I wanted to hear it from you.

6

Back to the present.

I found you in my locker the next morning.

6A

Not you.
A photograph.
But for a moment, it felt like finding a body.
It felt like finding
what ~~you~~ I needed
to be

found.

6B

6C

Not slipped into the locker through one of the airholes or through the crack in the bottom. No: taped up, white envelope. The photographer had broken into my locker and left it there for me.

6D

It brought you back to me.

The way you

said "I love you"

said "I'll never sleep with you"

said "I will always"

kept a list of all your favorite moments in a composition book and would underline the ones involving me with blue ink

~~screamed at me not to do it not to do it not to do it~~

believed that birds talked to you

~~slapped Jack slapped him slapped him slapped him~~

refused to eat any jelly beans but the black ones

cried when my cat Chester died more than I cried, even

helped me dig his grave

dug the grave

looked the most beautiful when

you didn't realize how beautiful you looked

the moments I would catch you thinking

~~always wondering if you were thinking of me, knowing sometimes you were~~

~~and sometimes you weren't~~

~~you weren't~~

I knew you better than anyone else. I was sure of it.

~~*Anything?*~~

~~*Something?*~~

But I had never seen this photo before.

6E

~~*I have never seen this photo before.*~~
~~*I have never seen this photo before.*~~

6F

I slammed my locker shut. Some people turned to look at me. I wondered if any of them was the one. If the photographer was watching me. Seeing my reaction. Recording it.

I crashed through the halls, crashed through my mind, crashed through all this mental history, crashed into people, crashed and felt the breaking—

Jack was talking to some of his friends from track. I didn't want to interrupt but if I didn't interrupt I knew I'd fall apart, so I tried to calm the crashing, tried to keep myself normal as I walked over and said, "Hey," and said, "Can I speak to you for a second?" and pulled him away from them because this involved you and I was sure the rest of them had all forgotten you by now and wouldn't understand why this was so urgent and how things had changed. I led Jack into an empty history classroom and let the door close behind us.

"What's up?" he asked.

~~*Up*, I thought.~~

"This," I said, looking down at the photo in my hand.

~~*Down*, I thought.~~

And Jack, who always kept so cool, ~~Jack, who had track friends—Jack, who told me all the time to move on—Jack, who you hadn't really loved like you loved me~~ Jack took one look at the photograph and gave me a glimmer of what I must have looked like. When you say someone looks "haunted," it doesn't matter if you're talking about the ghost or about the person who's seen the ghost. The expression is the same. It's a sudden constant death, and the haunting comes from the surprise.

"Where did you get this?" Jack asked. He left it in my hand. He wouldn't touch it.

"It was in my locker," I told him. "Someone put it there."

"Who?"

"I don't know."

"You don't know?"

"I don't know. Whoever it is knows my combination. They just put it right in."

"Well, who knows your combination?"

"Ariel's the only one."

~~I'd told you~~

~~*18—the age I'll be when I leave this place*~~

~~*two turns left*~~

~~*74—July 4th*~~

~~*one turn right*~~

~~*90—the number of bottles of beer on the wall after nine of them have fallen*~~

"She never told me," he said. "In case you're thinking she told someone."

"She's all dressed up," I said.

"I never saw her like that," he told me. "Nothing like that."

Even when I held it close, I couldn't tell if you were happy. Right in front of me, and I couldn't tell. As if that would have been the biggest clue to when it was.

~~Up or down? Were you in an up or a down?~~

"I would remember it," I said, as much to myself as to Jack. "I would remember her like this."

He reached for the photo, and I actually hesitated a second before giving it to him. As if he would destroy it. Or keep it for himself.

I wondered what he would tell his track friends about me pulling him away, or even if they'd ask. I'd always been insecure around him, but now it was amplified. I could never believe we were truly friends. It was as if he'd married into our friendship when he started going out with you. We weren't friends—we were stepfriends.

But with you gone, he was still the person I felt closest to.

I watched him as he stared at the photo. ~~At you.~~

"It's in the woods," he said finally. "She must've gone with someone else into the woods."

Neither of us.

Someone else.

I felt empty enough for both of us. And I imagined he felt empty enough for both of us. Which left us four times empty and none smarter.

"It's the same person who took the other pictures," he guessed. "But we don't know who that is."

I nodded.

"Jesus," he said. "This is completely messed up."

Are you sure it's not her? I wanted to ask. But I knew what he would say. That was our difference: There was part of me that *wanted* to be haunted, because at least that would be feeling something that radiated from you. But he was different: He had closed himself off, except when I came around to bring it all back.

"You have to help me," I said. ~~Because if I couldn't talk to you, I could at least talk to him in the same way I would've talked to you.~~

"Okay," he said. "Okay."

But then he didn't say anything else, and I knew it was up to me to figure out how to begin.

6G

That night, I spent hours staring at the photograph.

But you weren't telling me anything.

6H

I remembered a time we were going through magazines. There was this one model who looked icy to the touch, in total control. I told you that, and you said, "That's what makes it a good photograph. You think you know what's going on in her head. But the truth? No matter how good a photograph is, you can never tell what's going on in the person's mind. There's no way to get from here" (you pointed to the room) "to there" (you pointed to her head).

61

I was treating the past as if it could be mined for clues, for reasons.

But the past resists that.

It holds too much evidence of too many things.

7

You were the one who taught me how to spy on people. I guess, in many ways, that's how you met Jack.

It's not hard for me to remember that part. He'd go running after school, even when it wasn't track season. You and I would wander, and he kept crossing our path. Unlike most track teamers, who always took the same route, he would change his up as much as we'd change ours. I barely noticed it, but you did.

"It's that guy again," you'd say.

Then: "He's cute, you know."

~~*No, I don't know. And you don't need to tell me.*~~

It wasn't enough to pass him as we were heading to your house or cutting over to the library. Soon you had to have sightings in the halls, too. Then sighting turned into spying, and spying turned to stalking. You could tell me how many pairs of jeans he owned before you officially knew his name.

"I'm not sure he's our type," I told you.

"Our type?" you said back. "I didn't know we had a type."

I played along, but tried to get you to spy on other people with me. The teachers who were long past due for a meltdown, or the pompous student council president whose re-election bid was about to go down in flames. Misery—I was scoping out misery for us to witness. Then one day I had to stay late to make up a math quiz, and you walked home alone. This time when he ran by, you said hey. And he said hey back. ~~Leaving me to wonder for the rest of my life what would have happened if I had been there.~~

I didn't think ~~he~~ the two of you would last. I continued to play along, but it stopped feeling like play. ~~This is the thing they don't tell you about being a third wheel—it's not like you're the wheel that's added on. You were one of the original two wheels, but suddenly you're not so important anymore. The relationship drives fine without you.~~

"Don't worry," you'd tell me. "He'll never know me like you do."

But you told him the same thing, didn't you? He told me this, one night soon after. But by then, I guess it was beside the point.

7A

He was the one who got the next photo. This time it was bigger, and it was in his locker.

He found me at lunch and pulled me aside. And at first I didn't get what he was saying, and then I was just sad, because even though it was freaking me out, it had still felt special to have it only happening to me.

"It's a gravestone," I said when he showed it to me.

"Yeah, I know."

"I can't read it."

Jack looked at me funny then.

"Do you really not know what it is?" he asked.

I shook my head. I had no idea what he was talking about.

He tried to stare me down.

"Look, Evan, I need to know: Did you put this in my locker?"

"What do you mean?"

"If this is your kind of sick joke, that's fine. I know things have been messed up. But this crosses the line."

His accusation stung. At the very least, I thought we had trust.

"Jack," I said, "I didn't put it in your locker. I've never seen it before."

"She never told you?"

"Told me *what*?"

There must have been enough disbelief in my voice, because he relented a little.

"Never mind," he said.

"No. Tell me." ~~Even though it was in his locker, the photo was still at least partly mine.~~

"She never told you?"

"No." ~~You never told me what you saw in him. Not convincingly.~~

"This," he said, pointing at the gravestone, "is where she and I first kissed."

~~Did I tell you I didn't want to know? Or did you choose not to tell me?~~

Jack looked all messed up now, and I needed him not to be. Being messed up was my thing, not his.

"What the hell's going on?" he asked. "Is this about Miranda?"

I was confused. "Miranda?"

"Look, Ev—you know Miranda Lee?"

I nodded.

"We . . . well, we might be dating. I mean, I want us to be. And I think we are. We just haven't, you know, had the conversation yet."

"Oh."

"I was going to tell you."

"Why? I mean, you don't have to."

"C'mon, Ev. I was going to tell you. I mean, it's not anything yet. And it's not like I'm . . . I mean, it's been a while. And Miranda's really nice."

She was. Nice.

Part of me was happy for him. ~~Happy happy happy.~~ And part of me was just . . . surprised. It felt . . . ~~wrong sudden disloyal mean~~ I didn't know what it felt.

I didn't know what to say. So instead I held up the photo of the gravestone and told him, "You have to show me where it is."

7B

I didn't want to go after dark, but Jack's practice schedule left us no choice. ~~There is no such thing as no choice. There is always a choice. The only question is whether it's a bearable one.~~ The cemetery wasn't that far from where he lived, so I met him at his house. I stood awkwardly in the doorway as he made excuses to his parents, in the same way he'd made excuses to head out with you.

~~*"Are you two inseparable now?" I asked you.*~~

~~*You laughed. "Don't you know, Evan? People are always separable."*~~

~~*I wanted to say I had once thought the two of us were inseparable. But that would have only proven your point.*~~

We didn't talk on the way over. All the things I didn't want to ask him and all the things he didn't want to tell me added up to an unhelpful silence.

For a second, I pictured the two of you kissing. ~~One time I saw you. It was Gabe Weismann's party and you'd skipped to the backyard. I had gotten you a drink, even though you hadn't asked me to. I was looking for you, just to give you the drink. I didn't~~

~~see you in the shadows at first. You were kissing. It wasn't anything more than that. I felt so invisible. Because neither of you was seeing me. You were lost in each other. Not just the sight of each other. The feel. The taste. The contact. I was outside of it.~~

~~I wondered if Jack remembered that. I wondered if things like that haunted him now. I wondered what happened to kisses when they were over.~~

~~It's not like I could ask him this.~~

Finally, as we passed through the cemetery entrance, I said, "Tell me."

"Tell you what?"

"The story. You and Ariel. The first kiss. That's what this is about, isn't it?"

He sighed. ~~I was sure there were moments when he hated me.~~ "It seems like a really long time ago, right?"

I nodded.

"But I remember it. I don't know if that matters now."

"Tell me."

Why was I being so insistent? Mostly because it was making him so uncomfortable. Mostly because I'd never been sure if he'd registered any of it. I always felt it was unfair that even though both of us did what we did, I was the one who took on the suffering afterwards. ~~Do you blame us equally?~~

"There's not much to tell you," he said now, leading me to the gravestone in the picture. "She was having one of her up nights—she was all energy, bouncing around and telling me how happy she was. It felt good, you know? To be the guy making her happy. We'd gone to the movies, and then she said she'd walk me home. When we got to my house, she said she didn't want it to be over yet. She asked me what was around, and when I told her the cemetery, she said that was perfect. We got in here—just hopped over the wall; it's not that high. And she started running around, reading all of the inscriptions to me. *Beloved wife and mother*, that kind of thing. I tried to catch up with her, but when she was in one of those moods, it was impossible to catch up with her. Right? I'd chime in every now and then, but mostly it was her show. Then we got to this one, and she got quiet."

We were in front of the gravestone from the photo now. I tried to read it, but I couldn't. Time had worn away all of the words. Some light green moss grew on it instead.

"You can't read it anymore," I said. "That's what upset her."

Jack nodded. "She kept saying, 'What's the point? All this, and what's the point?' And I don't know—I just wanted to kiss her so much then. I wanted it, and she needed it. So I held her, and I kissed her, and we just started making out in the middle of a graveyard."

"That's so romantic," I said.

"What do you know about romance, Ev? I mean, really."

It took me by surprise, his anger. I hadn't realized he cared enough to be angry with me.

He took out a cigarette, looked at me for my permission, then lit it.

"Runner like you shouldn't dabble in cancer," I said, pressing my luck.

"You sound like her," he said, then let it hang there, like the smoke.

I looked around the gravestone for another envelope, but didn't find anything.

"Are you watching us?" I called out. "Anyone there?"

"This time of night," Jack said between drags, "they'd need a flash."

"*He'd* need a flash," I said. "Or she'd."

"Who is it, Evan? If it's not you and not me, who is it?"

"Do you think there was someone else? ~~Do you think she was cheating on you?~~"

"No. Did she have any other friends she would've told? ~~Do you think she was cheating on *you*?~~"

Between us, we were supposed to know you. Between us, we were supposed to know everything.

~~*"You have to help me," I said to him. "We have to help her."*~~

"We would joke about it," he continued. "That first kiss. How weird it was. I was going to find out whose grave it was. I was going to find out, and then on our anniversary, I was going to write the name back on. I thought she'd like that."

I looked down at the anonymous stone. I couldn't meet his eye.

"She needed help," I told him.

"Shame we couldn't give it to her."

I lifted my head to stare at him in the darkness, over the gravestone.

"Do you really believe that?" I asked.

"Some days I do. Some days I don't."

"She was breaking," I told him. "We had to."

"I'm not convinced we didn't break her more," he replied.

"You can't break someone by caring."

"Are you really sure about that?"

~~*"I don't need your help!" you screamed.*~~

~~*"Yes, you do," he told you. "Evan and I both think that."*~~

~~*"You're against me! Both of you—you're against me."*~~

~~*"That's not it," I said. "That's not it at all." But I wasn't sure you could hear me over your own crying.*~~

~~*"They'll be here soon," Jack said. "It's for the best."*~~

~~*I was glad he sounded so confident. Because I was starting to wonder whether we'd done the right thing.*~~

~~*"I'll kill myself. I swear, I'll kill myself," you threatened.*~~

~~*"We're not going to leave you alone," I said.*~~

~~*But we had to, eventually.*~~

~~*After all, people are always separable.*~~

"Evan?" Jack said to me now. "You there?"

"As much as I ever am."

I half expected him to follow up with *You okay?* But instead he started walking back home.

"There's nothing for us here," he called back to me. "I guess we'll just see what happens next."

"I'm not okay," I said.

But he was already too far away to hear me.

8

We had to face the fact: Someone else knew you. Maybe not another boyfriend or another best friend. But someone who would have known where you and Jack had your first kiss. Someone who would have followed you to the spot where it all happened. And took pictures.

8A

It wasn't like we didn't know other people. It wasn't like I sat alone at lunch now. But there are people you know, and there are people you have a connection with, and I had thought that you'd only had a connection with me and Jack. ~~Wasn't that what made us feel responsible—not for what happened, but responsible for you? We always felt responsible for you. That's the nature of connection—not just the attachment, but the responsibility.~~

At lunch, I sat with people from class ~~at a different table from the one I sat at with you~~. It was easier that way. Strangers were more difficult. One time, there was a field trip, and Matt, who I usually ate with, wasn't there. I sat at our usual table, and this girl sat down, looked at me, and said, "You were friends with the crazy girl, weren't you?" And I didn't know what to say. I kept eating, pretending I hadn't heard her. Finally she said, "You must be crazy, too," and then left to sit somewhere else.

The whole time, I didn't look up. But under the table, I crossed my legs so hard it hurt. I was using all the strength it would take to run away, only to stay still.

~~Was that how you felt?~~

8B

There weren't any new photos over the weekend, and there weren't any on Monday morning, either. ~~I felt like I was missing something. Missing you more. Missing whatever was going to happen next.~~

Monday at lunch I followed Matt from calculus, talking about homework and our history test and nothing that mattered. ~~You and I never talked about calculus.~~ There were football players sitting at our table, so Matt led me over to where Katie and that group were sitting. Katie had a camera out.

"What's that for?" I asked her.

She looked at me ~~strangely~~. "For taking pictures? For art class?"

Charlie chimed in with, "Do you want her to take your picture?"

"Oh, cut it out," Fiona said. "It was a perfectly valid question."

Katie's camera was new and digital and small—not the kind of camera I imagined had taken the photographs that Jack and I had gotten. So I didn't know how valid a question it had actually been.

~~*Valid questions:*~~

~~*Why am I still here?*~~

~~*Who are these people?*~~

~~*What should I say next?*~~

~~*Are they expecting me to say something next?*~~

Katie and Charlie were eating from the same cardboard boat of French fries. Matt was talking to Rich, another refugee from our usual table, about World of Warcraft. Fiona would take a look at us all, then take a bite of her sandwich, then take another look at us all. Which was pretty much the same thing I was doing, only I was eating a square slice of pizza.

She and I didn't have any classes together, so I didn't know what we could talk about.

"Do you like to take pictures?" she asked me.

"No," I said. Then I realized too late that I'd shut down the conversation. I had to think of something else to say.

"Do you?" I asked.

She shrugged. "When the mood hits me, I guess."

"When does the mood hit you?"

"I don't know. It's a mood."

~~I thought: *You don't understand that talking is hard for me. I watch all of you doing it, but I just can't. I could with her. But I can't now.*~~

"Evan?"

I looked up at Fiona. I hadn't realized I'd looked down. I hadn't realized she wanted me to say something else.

"Sorry," I said. "I was just . . . thinking."

"About what?"

"Nothing, really."

She looked disappointed.

"I'm sorry," I said again.

She smiled. "What do you have to be sorry about?"

~~*Ariel. The fact that I can't talk to you normally. The fact that you're being nice and I can't be nice back—not because I don't want to. I want to be nice. But my mind won't let me speak. My body won't let me speak. It's too uncomfortable.*~~

"Lots," I said.

Now Fiona looked at me a different way, and I wondered if this was how I used to look at you, the barely masked concern that lands like pity.

~~What was weird was: I thought I'd hidden it so well. I thought, to them, I was just quiet Evan, shy Evan, plain Evan. I was the orphan sidekick, the trusty wallflower.~~

"I gotta go," I said, even though my lunch wasn't finished and there were still at least fifteen minutes to go before next period. As I stood up, I had the strangest sensation that this would be the moment that someone would take a picture of, because this was the moment I'd least want to be captured.

~~You said that once, didn't you? I remembered it. One morning, I was at your locker and you were just staring inside it, as if there was a mirror there. "Ariel?" I asked. And you said, "Why is it that I'm always forced to see people at the exact time I don't want anyone to see me? Why is life that cruel?" Jack might have made a joke about it, but I took it seriously.~~

"Bye," Fiona said, and I managed to say it back. Even Matt was looking at me a little weirdly as I left; he'd noticed me talking to Fiona, and it was clear he thought it was a good thing, which I was now messing up. This only made me want to leave faster, and I almost spilled my soda on Katie's head as I swerved away. I liked them all, but I was going, and the only person I blamed was myself.

As I left, I saw Jack at his table, laughing with his friends. This feeling would always be mine alone.

8C

Between every period, I passed both my locker and Jack's, hoping to catch someone placing a photograph inside. I was waiting for it, really. I couldn't believe that he or she would stop.

At the end of the day, I found Jack putting his books away. I had come up with a plan.

"Anything?" I asked him.

"Nope," he said, closing the door.

"That doesn't make any sense," I said.

"I have to go to practice. I promise I'll tell you if something comes up."

He was about to walk away, and I felt I couldn't let him. Not yet.

"Doesn't it bother you?" I asked.

He looked at me impatiently. "What?"

"That she told someone else."

"It is what it is."

"No, there's something else there."

Jack slammed his hand against his locker door. "Look," he said. "What do you want me to do? What do you want me to say? There's a part of me that thinks you're actually *enjoying* this."

~~Enjoying. This.~~

"Jack~~—you can be such a jerk sometimes.~~"

"No—I know. That's not right. But, Evan, I don't know what you want from me here. It doesn't make any sense for us to get worked up over something we don't have any control over."

"I've thought about it," I said.

"And?"

"I think we need to go to her house."

He was not expecting me to say this.

"What are you talking about?"

"Think about it for a second. If she was close enough to someone to tell him or her our locker combinations and the place where you two first kissed—don't you think she would have mentioned that person in her journals?"

"Wait a second, Evan—"

"No, it makes perfect sense. All we have to do is read the journals—we don't even have to read them, we can just scan them. But there has to be a name there."

"Are you crazy?"

~~*"You must be crazy, too."*~~

"No."

"First of all, I don't think Ariel's parents would just let us into their house ~~because of what we did to their daughter~~. Second, we have no idea if the journals ~~that I don't want to read~~ are still there. And third . . . ~~I'm sick of you~~ well, it's just wrong."

"You remember where the spare key is, don't you? ~~You are not getting out of this.~~ I'm sure it's in the same place. Nobody ~~not even your new girlfriend~~ ever has to know we were there. *Nobody*. It's the only way for us to find out."

Jack shook his head. "No. We're not doing it. I'm late for practice."

"If you don't do it with me, I'm doing it alone," I told him.

Jack hit the locker again. "*Evan.*"

"Someone's stalking us," I said. "We have to stop it. The only way is to find out who it is. Her parents both work until six now, at the earliest. I've been by their house. They're never back before six." ~~This wasn't true. I was just guessing.~~

"Does it have to be tonight?"

~~I knew if I wavered, I'd lose him.~~

"Yeah. Let's get it over with."

Jack didn't like any of it, but he wasn't going to make me do it myself.

"Fine. ~~I think you're a jerk, too, sometimes.~~ I'll get out of practice early and meet you here at four. Out front. In the meantime, go over there and make sure their cars aren't in the garage."

I nodded and started to leave. But Jack grabbed my shoulder and turned me so I had to look him right in the eye.

"I'm only going to say this once, Evan, okay? If I find out that these are your photos and you're doing this just to mess with me, I'll kill you. Got it?"

"Don't worry," I told him. "I'm not that smart. Or that masochistic."

He let me go.

"I think you are that smart," he said. "But not that cruel. That's what I'm betting on."

This was, I figured, the biggest compliment he'd ever paid me.

9

I let myself lose focus as I walked over to Ariel's house. There were so many frequencies playing in my mind.

"I'm having sex with him," you said. "You know that, right?"

"It was a perfectly valid question," Fiona said.

"I guess I did," I said.

~~*I didn't. I didn't want to think about it.*~~

"Mrs. Taylor, you have to come with me now."

"I don't know. It's a mood."

"Evan, get help. I'll stay here. You get help."

~~*But I wanted to be the one to stay.*~~

"My parents aren't home right now," Fiona said.

~~*No. Not Fiona.*~~

"What is it, Evan? What is it?"

~~*It's the end. It's the end. I can't stop it.*~~

~~*"I am so happy right now," you said.*~~

~~*You wanted to die.*~~

~~*I have to stop thinking about these things.*~~

~~*"It's Ariel. She's—"*~~

"Make sure their cars aren't in the garage."

Checked. Check. Checklisted. Checked off. Checkmate.
~~*"I'm not in love with you."*~~

9A

Your red bike was still there. It's not like you ever rode it. So it made sense that it was still there.

I was going to tell Jack that, but by the time it was four o'clock, I'd forgotten.

9B

On our way over, I asked him, "Are you sure you want to do this?"

He was speechless for a second, then said, "I tell you, Evan, sometimes I don't understand you at all."

9C

~~I came with the territory.~~
~~What was the territory?~~

9D

~~*"I'm not in love with you."*~~

9E

The key was right where I knew it would be. I'd never used it, but I'd seen you use it all the time. You never carried your own key. You just used the one hidden in the lip of the geranium pot.

~~*"Come on," you said. We were supposed to be studying. I can't remember what. And I thought,* Okay, here we are. *It was what? October or November of tenth grade? Before Jack. Before*~~

Jack and I let ourselves in the back door. I went to turn on the light, but Jack told me not to.

"Wait till we get to her room," he said. "Less chance of someone seeing it."

~~*"Let's just go to my room," you said. We didn't bother turning on any of the lights. You led me by my hand.*~~

It was starting to sink in now: We were in your house. It smelled like your house, a little bit like pillows and a little bit like pine. There were the same magnets on the refrigerator, the same paintings on the walls. ~~Do you miss them?~~ It made me realize it hadn't been all that long ago, when things had changed. And just because people changed, it didn't mean houses automatically changed, too.

Jack had fallen quiet, but he was looking around as much as I was.

"It's weird," I said.

He nodded.

Jack and I had never been in your house without you. We'd never waited here for you to show up, never hung around while you ran off to do something. I'm sure there were times when we'd been watching a movie and you'd left us alone on your lime-green couch to go get something. But I couldn't remember any of those times now. I couldn't remember ordinary moments, only the ones that had made an impression. Ordinary moments were the ones that fell away first.

~~*You opened the door. You lit some candles. You left the lights off.*~~

Your door was closed, and I had this ~~stupid~~ moment when I wondered if we should knock.

~~*"Make yourself comfortable," you said, so I went to the bed. Kicked off my shoes. Made myself comfortable there.*~~

Neither of us wanted to be the one to open the door. We just stood there until Jack finally grabbed the knob and turned.

It was still your room, but it was different. ~~*Anything. Something.*~~ Someone besides you had cleaned it. Everything was in place, which wasn't like you at all. ~~*Anything. Something.*~~ It was as if the whole room had been folded neatly. ~~One more betrayal.~~

~~*Anything.*~~

~~*Something.*~~

~~*Nothing.*~~

Suddenly I was light-headed, like I hadn't eaten in weeks. I sat down on the bed. ~~*I made myself comfortable.*~~ Feeling it under me made me want to cry.

~~*You crawled in next to me. We were supposed to be studying. And there, in the flicker of the candlelight, I guess we were. I studied you. You studied me. You smiled. I was too lost to smile.*~~

"Hey, Evan," Jack said, "don't lose it. Let's just get what we came for and leave."

I couldn't believe this was easy for him. I couldn't believe he wasn't shaken, too. I didn't know why, but this got to me just as much as being in your ~~dead~~ room. Before I could think about it, I was yelling at him, "What do you know, Jack? *What do you know about anything?*"

The tears were coming, but I was too angry to cry. They just fell out of my eyes.

"That's not fair, Evan," Jack said, standing in front of the bed.

"I'm so sorry *it's not fair.*"

He sighed. "Evan, you should talk to someone about this. Really, you need to talk to someone."

"How about you, jerk?" I said. "Why can't I talk *to you* about it?"

~~The first time the three of us went to the movies together, he waited until you went to get popcorn, and then he said, "You don't mind, do you?" And I'd been so moved that he'd asked, that he wanted my permission.~~

"Do you really think this is the time and place? We're in her room, Ev."

"Yeah," I said. "Don't you think that's a little weird? Doesn't that *disturb* you?"

He looked at me ~~like I was out of my mind~~. "*Of course it does.* Jesus, who do you think I am?"

"You never talk about it," I said. "Ever."

"What is there to talk about, Evan? It's done. She's gone. It happened. We did the right thing. Is that what you want to hear? Well, we did. We did the right thing."

~~I hated that I needed him so much. Because he was the only one who knew.~~

"I wasn't sure I'd ever be in here again," he said, staying in the perfect middle of the room, as if he didn't want to touch anything. "It all feels so empty now, doesn't it? It's like her spirit's gone. So it's just a room. And that's so completely surreal. I know you think I don't care about it, but that's not true. I'm just not as open as you, okay? That's how I deal with it. But that doesn't make this easier. I don't want to be here, Evan—and I can't help but feel that you do. It's your way of keeping things going even after they've stopped."

"They haven't stopped," I told him. "Even with her gone, things don't stop. As long as we're around, they'll keep going."

"Remember at the beginning, when we fought it? When we said we weren't going to let go of her?"

~~*I studied you. You studied me. We lay there. I moved my hand gently onto your arm.*~~

I nodded. "Yeah, that didn't work."

Finally, he touched something—a picture frame, with you and your parents safely inside. "I don't think they'd be very happy to find us here," he said.

~~*"It's not your fault," your mom had said that first night. But she never said it again.*~~

"I like to think Ariel knows we're here," I said. "That somehow she senses it. Wherever she is."

~~*I moved my hand gently onto your arm.*~~

Jack put down the photo. "That's assuming she's forgiven us."

~~*"Evan," you said. "Don't fall in love with me, okay?"*~~

"Yeah. I guess so."

~~*"I'm not in love with you," I said.*~~

I looked at your mirror, which was surrounded by more photos. Some of you and Jack. Some of you and me. A couple of Jack alone. One of me alone. Only one of Jack and me together, from Six Flags in May.

~~*You didn't move your arm. You let me rest there. You didn't pull away. You pulled closer. You were so good to me. You knew and pretended you didn't.*~~

~~*"Let's always love each other, and never be in love with each other."*~~

~~*And I agreed.*~~

"Evan?" Jack said.

I pointed to the picture from Six Flags. "That was a good day, wasn't it?"

And then . . .

"What's that?" I asked, pointing to the picture next to it.

Jack didn't see it at first—it was small compared to the other snapshots, the same size as the first photo I'd received.

"Look," he said, taking it out of the mirror frame and handing it to me.

9F

9G

"It has to be the same photographer," he said.

I looked at it closely.

"Is that Ariel?" I asked.

"I think so. I'm not sure, but I think it is."

"On the railway bridge."

"Walking on the tracks. Jesus."

"You don't think she was—"

"Trying to kill herself? Doesn't look like it. And it would have to be one scary individual to take photos of a suicide attempt."

"It's like she's floating there. Like she's already dead."

"Ariel the angel, huh?"

That sounded dumb. "Not really," I mumbled.

"You see," Jack said, taking the photo back from me, "I don't think it looks like she's floating at all. I think she's teetering. Which is just about right. It's shaky because she's about to fall."

~~*The train comes. If you stay on the tracks, you die. If you jump off the bridge, you die.*~~

"So who took it?" I asked.

~~*There's always a train coming eventually.*~~

"Well, that's the question, isn't it? If I remember correctly, we're here to find that out."

"The journals," I said.

"Yeah, the journals."

I knew you kept them in a box under your bed. I knew that because I'd seen you take one out, write in it, then put it away. I'd never looked in the box, and had certainly never read anything you'd written. That would have been the worst kind of violation, to read your words uninvited. Now, though, it was like all those rules were off.

I reached down for the box *~~I'm sorry~~*, and Jack said, "Wait." I looked back up at him. He was even more skittish than before. ~~You made him afraid. Did you realize how afraid you made him?~~

"I understand why we're doing this," he said, "and I'm okay with you checking to see if she, you know, mentions someone else. But I don't want to read it. Any of it. And I don't want you to tell me. Because we don't know what she wrote there. And if she said anything about me that I'm not ready to hear—well, I don't know if I'll ever be ready to hear it. I need to remember it the way I'm remembering it now. If that's all a lie, I don't want to know it."

I looked at him. How helpless he was.

"She loved you," I said. "You know that, right? She loved you."

And that's what did it. That's what made the tears finally come to his eyes.

"You can't know that for sure," he said quietly.

"Yeah, I can. There are only a few things I know for sure, and that's one of them. There's not going to be anything in the journals that disputes that. I'm sure there were times when she was mad at you. And there were definitely times she was out of her head. But on the base level, she loved you."

~~It was hard to say these things. I knew he wouldn't say them back. I had to trust my belief that you loved me, too. In a different way. We were never in love. But we loved each other.~~

As he wiped his eyes, looking mad at himself for letting something out, I reached under the bed and found the box. It was surprisingly light as I pulled it out. Then I took a look inside and saw why.

It was empty.

9H

My mind became a brief history of empty boxes.

The big cardboard ones I'd find as a kid and turn into a fort. Or a house, drawing in windows on the sides. I would cut out the windows and ruin it.

Boxes that sweaters would come in. Boxes from department stores that I would keep in the bottom of my closet until they could be filled with some kind of collection.

Coffins.

The Cracker Jack box when I was all done, when the prize had been revealed to be something plastic, something worthless.

An empty sandbox, looking like it was waiting for sand.

A mailbox always looks like it's full of envelopes. But you never know for sure. Most of the time when you open it, it sounds hollow.

What did Pandora do with her box after she'd unleashed despair into the world? Did she keep it on her mantel, as a reminder of what she'd done?

91

I threw the empty box aside. I crawled under your bed, looking for another box. Looking for something, for the prize. And when I didn't find it, I was suddenly so angry at everything. I started ripping at things. Your room was not supposed to be neat. I pulled at the sheets until the mattress was bare. I attacked the drawers by the handles. Jack was yelling at me to stop. He was asking me what I was doing. I was sick of emptiness, tired of order. I opened the drawers one by one, looking for those journals, looking for any word from you.

"Evan!" Jack was shouting. He grabbed at my arms, but I pushed him off. ~~*I was just like you.*~~

I reached the bottom drawer of your desk. I reached for the bottom drawer of your desk. I pulled it open.

You know what I found there, don't you?

9J

9K

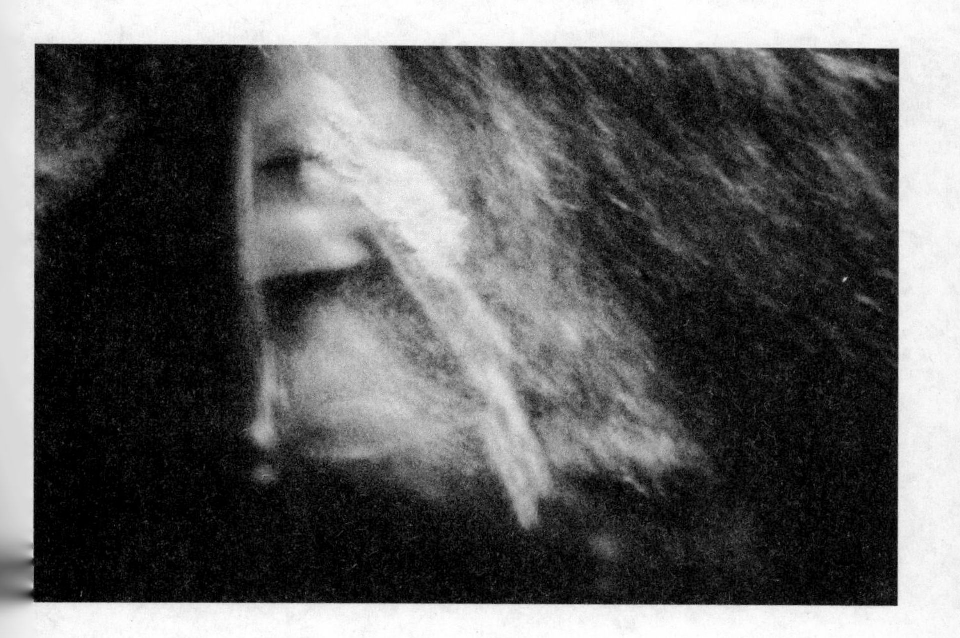

9L

9M

9N

I turned them over. There were dates and captions on the back. Months ago. ~~Before.~~ It wasn't your handwriting.

11/11 tracks
11/11 underneath
11/11 Sparrow
11/14 self-portrait

As quickly as I'd started trashing the place, I stopped. Jack was back in action now, first staring at me, then staring at the pictures in my hand.

"It's the guy," Jack said. "That's him."

I turned over the photo. "It says it's Sparrow." I held up the abstract fourth picture. "This is the self-portrait."

"Well, that's a big help."

I studied the captions. "It looks like a girl's handwriting," I said.

"Still, there's a guy. Right here."

I didn't see what Jack was so bothered by. "I really don't think that's a self-portrait," I said.

"Yeah, but she kept a picture of him, Evan. You don't keep a picture of a total stranger."

"It was in her drawer. It's not like she had it up."

"But maybe she wanted to keep him a secret, okay? Maybe he's a secret."

~~*No*, I wanted to say. *She was ours*.~~

"There's no way he goes to our school," I said. "Even with two thousand kids, you'd remember that hair."

The air was getting dark; night was blooming. I opened the rest of the drawers in the room, more gently this time, but couldn't find anything else. No image. No word.

"We should go," Jack said. "Clean up and go."

~~*Go go go go go go go go*. Why is it such a short word? Shouldn't it be the same length as *STOP*?~~

I held up Sparrow's picture.

"People will remember him," I said. "Someone will recognize him. He's the key."

10

I never kept a calendar.

I had no idea what I'd been doing on 11/11. Or 11/14.

Had I been with you? For at least part of it? Had you seen Jack? Were you off with people we didn't know? Or people we did know?

I tried to remember other people. I tried to remember other people in your life. ~~*"My secret girlfriend," you joked.*~~ But nothing was there. Nothing I could reach. ~~*Or was it "my secret boyfriend"?*~~

I was starting to think I was making up memories, just to have answers.

Our brain does that sometimes.

Or at least mine does.

You were never able to trick yourself like that, were you?

10A

What had I given you that you could keep? ~~Not photographs. Other things.~~

Words and words and words and words. Mostly in person, or on the computer.

I should have given you my own ink.

~~*Why? So you would have had more to leave behind?*~~

I hadn't looked in your room for the roses, but I figured I would have seen them if they'd been there. ~~Do you remember?~~ It had been our arbitrary anniversary. Last year, near the end of the school year, so probably June.

"We don't have an anniversary," you'd said as we walked home from school. "We should have an anniversary."

"How about today?" I said. "If we're going to have an arbitrary anniversary, it might as well be today. We'll be celebrating the anniversary of the day we came up with our arbitrary anniversary."

You'd smiled. "I like that. I like that a lot."

We gave each other two hours to plan. Then we'd go to Brookner Park to celebrate.

I'd never given anybody flowers before, but I'd always wanted to. So I went into town, to the florist, and I got roses. I didn't want red ones, because it wasn't like this was a romantic anniversary ~~("except in the poetry sense," you would have added)~~. So I went with a dark yellow—the color of the sun just before it turns orange. I had them wrapped, and signed a card and everything. After that, I went out and bought some of your favorite foods—peach salsa, lemon yogurt, almond cookies. Then, since I'd covered the anniversary, I stopped in a couple more stores for the arbitrary part. Salad tongs. A gobstopper. Birdseed. ~~Somethings.~~

I was ten minutes early to the park and you were ten minutes late. This was about our usual ratio. You were rushed, flustered.

"I stopped at home and—oh my God—it was like I couldn't get back out, because Mom was home early, and she was asking me about homework, and it's like she thought I was still in seventh grade, so when I went to go back out, she was all like, 'Where are you going?' and I told her I was going out, and she was like, 'I can see that,' and I just didn't know what to say, you know? I knew there was something to say, but I just didn't know what it was. So instead of making it better, I left, and I'm sure when I get back, she's going to be seething. I swear, that house keeps getting smaller and smaller. Soon it's going to be an exquisite birdcage."

~~You were quiet with other people. This wasn't your usual talking. This was you with me.~~

I held the flowers out to you. ~~Remember?~~

"Happy arbitrary anniversary," I said.

Your eyes grew wide and you put your hand over your mouth.

"What?" I asked.

"I totally forgot our arbitrary anniversary, honey!"

For a second, I believed you. Then you laughed.

"Just kidding."

You reached into your pocket and pulled out a small box, the kind that rings come in.

I handed you the flowers and you handed me the box.

I held my breath a little as I opened it. I remember that.

"I figured each of our arbitrary anniversaries can have a theme. So this will be our Cat's Eye anniversary."

Inside the box was a marble, a bigger-than-usual marble. Completely black glass.

Cat's Eye.

I gave you everything I'd collected, but none of it seemed to add up to that single marble.

It was a good night. We talked, joked. Jack called a couple of times, but you didn't answer. Nobody else called. I couldn't remember anybody else ever calling, except your parents.

~~*Nobody else.*~~

When the time came for us to head home, I noticed that the roses were already wide open. They wouldn't last much longer than the day.

"Sorry about that," I said. "They were closed tighter in the shop."

"That's okay," you told me. "I like them better when they're dried up. I'll keep them for years. Until our Get Rid of the Roses anniversary."

And I kept the Cat's Eye. Until it disappeared.

~~Did you steal it one day when you were in my room? Or did I lose it? Either way, isn't it my fault for not noticing?~~

Why was I thinking about this?

Oh, yes—the roses.

Something to keep.

Something gone.

11

Jack and I had an advantage over the photographer: We had four photographs she didn't know we had. ~~I was assuming it was a she because handwriting doesn't lie.~~

But, of course, the advantage meant nothing if we didn't know what to do with it.

11A

I took Sparrow's photo to lunch. There was no way Jack could have asked his friends about it—it would be too out of character; there would be too many questions. So I was left showing it to my friends. They wouldn't think there was anything out of the ordinary about me being out of the ordinary. I didn't tell them where I'd gotten it—I just said I was wondering if any of them had seen this guy around. And as they responded, I couldn't help thinking about you ~~you you~~ and how they knew you.

Matt ~~was actually your first boyfriend—or "first ex-boyfriend," as you would tease him. In fifth grade. Or maybe sixth. It lasted a few months, just so you could get something from him for Valentine's Day. I think it was over on February 15th. He would tease you about it, even when you weren't in the mood for teasing. He couldn't tell the difference.~~ said, "Dude, look at that hair! I've never seen anyone at this school try that out."

Fiona ~~had been friends with you—maybe even good friends—until you started spending all your time with Jack and, to a lesser extent, me. She was shaken after everything that happened, but not to the point that she felt the guilt as well as the shock.~~

studied the picture for a while. Then she turned it over, read the caption, and handed it back to me. "Nothing," she said. "Sorry."

Katie ~~thought you were a downer. She even said it to me once, shortly before: "I just can't spend too much time with her. She's a downer." I give her points for being the one to admit it. But did she ever ask herself why?~~ said, "He kind of looks like you. Not the hair, *obviously*. But there's something about him that reminds me of you."

Charlie ~~was drunk one time and asked me why I wasn't the one sleeping with you. That's how he put it.~~ told Katie she was out of her mind. But he didn't recognize Sparrow, either.

Who else would know? When you were here, in this cafeteria, ~~*Please come back. Please.*~~ you'd usually sit with Jack and his friends. When he talked to you, you seemed to fit in, but when someone else was talking, or he would be distracted, you just looked lonely over there. At least to me. ~~But whenever I would tell you that, you'd say, "I'm fine. I just slip out of it, you know?" And I'd say, "I'll catch you," and you would say, "It's not the kind of slipping you can catch."~~

"Where did you get that?" Fiona asked. She wasn't staring at the photograph—her green eyes were focused on me, only me. "If it was your photo, you'd know who was in it."

"I found it," I said, knowing how lame this sounded. "In the hall. I figured whoever it was would want it back."

"I still think it looks like you," Katie said.

"Whatever," Charlie said.

I felt foolish for trying. And part of me wanted to give in to the foolishness—to make copies of the photos and hang them around the halls like Wanted posters—asking *Have you seen this man?* Maybe offering a reward. As a way of solving this ~~uncertainty~~ mystery. Only, if I did that, the photographer would know. She would see it, and she would retreat. She'd cover her trail. ~~*You and I are walking in the snow. "Why are you walking backwards?" I ask. You point in the direction we came from. "So they'll think that's where I'm going." You point to where we're going. "And that's where I'm from."*~~

I changed the conversation. I thought I'd gone unnoticed. But after school, Fiona tracked me down.

"What are you doing?" she asked.

I shoved my books in my locker. Closed it.

"What do you mean?" I said.

"You've been weird for a week now. Something's going on."

"I don't know what you're talking about," I mumbled. Then I realized I was staring at the ground, not her. She'd never believe me if I didn't look at her. So I did, and the expression on her face was part pity, part annoyance, part understanding.

"It's like—" she said. Then stopped.

"What? What is it like?" I asked.

11B

That night, I broke about a hundred promises to myself and looked at your ~~old~~ online profile. I thought maybe there'd be some answers there. Or evidence.

It said your last log-in was the day in the clearing. You must've checked it before we went to school. Before the three of us left to hang out. Before.

~~Fiona's expression didn't change. "It's like right before it happened with Ariel, Evan. I know I wasn't there, but I was around it. I saw things. I remember how overwhelmed you were."~~

~~"It's not like that," I argued.~~

It was painful to see you frozen like that, frozen in time. It wasn't like you were smiling in your profile picture, or even happy—even though there were times you were happy ~~*anything something*~~ and there were times you were smiling ~~*kittens! playing poker!*~~; you just weren't the type to parade them. Instead it was a shot I had taken of you leaning against my bed, staring me down.

~~I'd been so excited when you chose it for your profile pic. So honored. Ridiculous.~~

I clicked on that picture to see more pictures.

~~"Then what's it like? What's going on?" Fiona asked.~~

~~There was no way for me to tell her. Because I felt that if I told her one thing, I'd have to tell her everything in order to explain it. Everything.~~

I could feel all the memories pressing against the ~~leaky~~ wall I'd put up to hold them back. The pressure was enormous, and I had to throw my body up against it ~~in my mind, this was all in my mind~~ so the memories didn't drown me. I was not going to look at the familiar pictures ~~*the parties*, *making faces into the camera phone*, *the birthdays*, *the two of us*~~—I was looking for something unfamiliar, something I hadn't noticed before.

~~"Evan," Fiona said, not reaching out with her hand, but with her voice, "I'm on your side."~~

~~"But who's on the other side, Fiona?" I had to ask. "Is it her? Does that mean you're against her?"~~

~~Fiona pulled back. "Evan, something's wrong with you. Even if nobody else can see it, I can see it."~~

I found one. Three weeks before it happened. A couple of days after the photos we found in your house.

The fingernail wasn't yours.

But the skin with the heart . . . the skin with the heart . . .

~~"I'm not saying there isn't something wrong," I told Fiona. I was tired. It felt like years of tiredness. "But you can't help." Because she wasn't there the last time, was she? "Really, it's nothing. I really have to go."~~

I didn't know. I couldn't remember.

~~Now Fiona risked it. She reached out. Put her hand on my shoulder. Squeezed. Said, "You don't have to do anything. You don't. It's over."~~

It was like I had never seen you before. Not in that one spot.

How can we remember every part of the body? Even on someone we love?

~~Fiona waited for a response. Not even an answer. A response.~~

There was no tag on the photo. No comments. No signs.

~~“It’s never over,” I said. “It can’t be.”~~

~~And I walked away.~~

11C

I spent the rest of the night scouring your profile. I didn't play music or say a word, so the only sounds my parents would hear, if they woke up, would be the light click of my fingers pressing the keys.

~~I remembered setting up our profiles together. How we had no idea that the random things we typed down in a single moment would then linger for years, mostly because we were too lazy to change them. That one snapshot of favorites, of self-description. For relationship status, we said we were married to each other. But eventually we changed that.~~

I went through all your other photos, but there weren't any surprises there. Then I looked at your comments page. Even after what happened, it remained active—in the days and weeks after, people wrote down that they missed you, that they prayed for you, that they remembered you. Even Jack. I was shocked to see his name and face there. And his comments.

FEB 11, 2:12 AM

come home

FEB 15, 12:22 AM

miss you

FEB 25, 3:02 AM

I'm sorry

FEB 25, 3:10 AM

Forgive me

As if you were reading it. ~~Could you see it? Was there any way?~~ As if he was going to get you back. ~~Not *Forgive us* but *Forgive me*.~~

I scrolled back to before. I saw the comments I'd left.

JAN 11, 6:20 PM

Whatre you doing Saturday? I have something fun we could do.

JAN 13, 11:11 AM

Hey, Drama Girl. This is Comedy Boy telling you to
"turn that frown upside down" (erg erg erg)

JAN 21, 11:13 PM

You still up? Call call call.

JAN 21, 12:05 AM

The sound of your voice = contentment.

~~*If only you knew, Comedy Boy. If only I could tell you.*~~

I looked on the days ~~11/11, 11/14~~ when the photos were

taken, but there weren't any comments that were out of the ordinary. Just me and Jack and two from Fiona and one from this guy Kilmer, who was always trying to convince you to ~~leave Jack~~ do yoga with him.

When I felt the comments were going to overwhelm me, I moved on to the friends page. You had 232 friends—maybe half of whom you'd actually met. I was looking for Sparrow, looking for some clue. First I checked out the profiles of the people I knew, the people from our school. Even with my friends, it had been a while since I'd read their whole pages—usually it was just the updates. There were things on there I didn't know and probably should have—Matt's favorite bands, or the fact that Fiona used to go to school in Georgia before she moved here. I clicked on all of their photos, hoping for some kind of intersection, but none of the mysterious photos appeared. If there were any pictures of you, they were offhand, refracted. You never looked absolutely the same—it was like every picture brought out a slight variation. I wondered if it was just because it was a different moment, or maybe each photographer brought out a different you—you could not be who you were without taking into account who was watching. I thought of what you'd say ~~*every you, every me*~~ and then stopped thinking about it. It was too hard.

Instead I thought about the word *profile* and what a weird double meaning it had. We say we're looking at a person's profile online, or say a newspaper is writing a profile on someone, and we assume it's the whole them we're seeing. But when a photographer takes a picture of a profile, you're only seeing half the face. ~~Like with Sparrow, whoever he was.~~ It's never the way you would remember seeing them. You never remember someone *in profile*. You remember them looking you in the eye, or talking to you. You remember an image that the subject could never see in a mirror, because you are the mirror. A profile, photographically, is perpendicular to the person you know.

I turned to the people I didn't know on your profile. People you had once known who'd moved away. Or people you'd met over summers, or online. You could have one conversation with someone because you liked the same band, and then they'd linger on, attached to you, forever. I read where they lived ~~California London Florida Montreal Chicago~~, and even though I knew they wouldn't have flown in to leave photos in my locker, I checked out who their friends were and what their photo albums looked like. I should have felt like I was knowing you more by learning about all these people, but instead I felt I was knowing you less and less. *She might not have really known these people*, I tried to ~~convince~~ remind myself.

It was three in the morning, and I was looking at the profile for a girl named Kelly in California. She loved the Beatles, Alice Walker, her two cats, and a mix of bad teen drama and bad reality TV. I clicked on her friends, moved to the second page . . . and there he was.

11D

11E

Sparrow. Only that wasn't the name underneath.

It was Alex.

I clicked on Alex's profile. It said he lived in the same town in California as Kelly. That made no sense to me. Hadn't he been here? I clicked on another of his friends. Same school, same town. So it couldn't be a lie.

Then I clicked on his photos.

And I found you.

And him.

And her.

11F

11G

11H

11

11J

~~*Ariel, look at me.*~~

~~*Look at me.*~~

~~*Look at me.*~~

11K

I sat there in the dark, staring at you. The screen was the only light on in the room, so I imagined your image projected into every corner. I was seeing it, but I was also within it. That last photo, you a blur. I was a blur, too. I was being erased because I would not stop for time.

11L

You see a photograph and you try to make yourself be there. But you can't. Even if you were there. You can't.

And if you weren't there, you retreat into desperate invention. You weave your own fiction and try to convince yourself it's fact.

It doesn't work.

A photograph is a souvenir of a moment.

It is not a moment.

It is the looking at the photograph that becomes the moment. Your own moment.

I was losing myself in there.

Because.

Because.

Because you were ~~everlasting in sunshine curious all right~~ the kind of beautiful that I remembered.

~~*"Let's go into the woods and take some pictures," you said. "I found this old camera."*~~

~~*"Let go!" you screamed. "Let go of me!"*~~

~~*"You have to let go," the counselor told me. "Let go of what you're holding inside."*~~

~~I can touch the picture but it's not your face.~~

~~I can touch the screen but it's not your face.~~

~~*Let go.*~~

11M

I pulled back and remembered what I was doing. ~~Investing~~ Investigating.

I looked at the dates Alex/Sparrow had posted the photo—11/13.

And there she was.

The photographer. Untagged. Nameless.

And I had no idea

none

who she was.

All this time, I thought if I could glimpse her, I would know.

I checked all of Alex/Sparrow's profile. I checked all of his friends for someone who looked like her. I went back and checked all of Ariel's pictures, all of Ariel's friends.

No recognition.

No similarities.

She knew me, but I didn't know her.

So then I did something ~~stupid~~. I didn't think about it. I just did it.

I sent Alex/Sparrow a message.

11N

How do you know Ariel?

110

It was morning already. At least where I was.

In California, I imagined Alex/Sparrow was still sleeping, postponing all my answers with his dreams.

12

I was waiting for Jack with printouts the next morning.

He looked annoyed to see me there in the smoking section, outside school. He checked for permission and lit his cigarette before saying anything.

"What is it now?" he finally asked.

~~I wondered what would have happened if we'd met up like this before you went over the edge. Would we have been able to stop you if we'd talked about it?~~

"I think I know who the photographer is," I told him.

I showed him the photos.

"Who is she?" he said.

"I don't know."

He looked at me hard. "I thought you just said you knew."

"Well, I know what she looks like. She's right there. Do you recognize her?"

"She looks familiar." He studied the photo some more. "But I couldn't tell you where from. Maybe she goes here. But maybe she just reminds me of someone."

I thought of Venn diagrams, those two overlapping circles.

And how the translation of "You remind me of someone" is that piece in between, that common space that's the only piece we're seeing.

"I didn't sleep last night," I told him. "I was up all night looking at her profile. Looking for Sparrow and this girl."

"I don't know who she is," Jack said, handing the photo back to me. "Sorry."

I found myself saying, "I wish she had a sister."

"What?"

I didn't know why I'd thought Jack would understand. Too often I thought he'd have the same impulses as me, just because we'd both loved you.

"If Ariel had a sister," I explained, "we could ask her. Show her the photos. Because we can't do that with her parents. They hate us."

"I don't think they—"

"They do, Jack. They hate us."

~~We went to your house the week after. To hear the news firsthand, instead of through gossip and rumors. They let us into the house, but it was clear that they didn't want us to stay there. They told us what the doctors said. It was what we'd already feared.~~

Jack ground out his cigarette and put his hand on my shoulder.

"Ev, I don't know what to tell you. We don't even know if it's the same girl who's leaving the pictures for us. Don't you think if these people were really important to Ariel, she would've told us about them?"

I was calmer now that he was using words like *we* and *us*.

~~I'd felt that way with you, too. Whenever you talked about *we* and *us*, I felt things made sense, that we were going through everything together, that if I could take it, then I could carry you through. It was only when you splintered off into your own lost *I* that things became complicated, overwhelming.~~

~~*"I don't know where I am, Evan."*~~

~~*"I'm seeing red everywhere. It's just . . . everywhere."*~~

~~*"I am underwater right now. You don't understand. I'm underwater."*~~

~~*"I need a gun."*~~

~~*"Evan? I need—"*~~

"Evan?"

Jack was waving his hand in front of me.

"*Evan.*"

"What?"

"Don't do that!" He was angry. "Jesus, not you, too, okay? Not you, too."

We just stood there for a moment, neither of us knowing what to say next. ~~Just like old times.~~ And then a girl asked, "Is this a bad time?"

"Hey, Miranda," Jack said, his tone lightening.

I didn't know whether to say hi or not. Miranda Lee wasn't someone I usually said hi to. She'd never been mean to me or nice to me or anything. She'd never been anything to me. She was one year younger than us and played sports, which was probably how Jack knew her.

"Hi," she said to both of us. "What's going on?"

I still had the photos out. I quickly put them back in my bag.

"Evan was just showing me some of his pictures," Jack explained smoothly ~~keeping you a secret~~. "He's working on a project. It's pretty cool."

"Cool," Miranda echoed.

"Yeah, thanks," I said. "Anyway, thanks for taking a look, Jack. I guess I'll be going. I mean, I was already going, so it's not you that's making me go, Miranda. I don't want you to think that."

"Oh, good," Miranda said. She didn't sound sarcastic. ~~If I'd said something like that to you, you would have been merciless. You had no use for sputtering.~~

I spent the next fifteen minutes before school walking the halls, looking for the photographer. I saw girls with similar hair or similar clothes or similar features, but never at the same time. Either she wasn't here, or she was hiding, or I wasn't looking right.

I had no way to know.

12A

~~When I walked through the halls, I thought of you. I wondered what you thought of this school now. This building. Was it a shelter against everything else? Could you be happy here? Or was it just another form of prison, just another place where you felt the weight of all the stones, all the people, all the thoughts?~~

~~I wish I'd known what was wrong with you.~~

~~I still wish I knew what was wrong with you.~~

12B

I felt weird asking my friends at lunch about another photo, when I'd just cross-examined them about Sparrow the day before. So I decided to wait.

Fiona, though, brought the whole thing up.

"Did you find Mr. Mohawk?" she asked.

"I think he's in California," I mumbled.

"You sent the detectives all the way to California?" Charlie joked.

"No, I found him online."

That should have been the end of the conversation. And it was—for everyone except Fiona.

"Who is he?" she asked.

"It doesn't matter," I said. Then I stood up from the table. "I have to run to the library. I almost forgot."

Fiona looked at my tray. "You haven't eaten anything."

I shrugged. "I'm not really hungry."

12C

Really: I was hungry. And I was remembering one of the things you had said. Not the last day in the woods, but maybe three days before. Everyone was supposed to hang out together, but you didn't want to go.

"Why?" I'd asked.

"I don't trust any of them," you'd said. "I don't trust Fiona. I don't want to see them. They think they know the truth, but they don't. I know the truth. They don't."

~~*The truth*. Really *the Truth*.~~

I should have been concerned. But then you'd said, "You're the one I trust. You." And that's what I felt. That's what I remembered.

12D

The day it happened, the week after it happened—those were not times I wanted to go back to. How I felt like I was trapped in a chamber of my own noise. Sitting in class and not being there at all. Sitting in a chair and fragmenting at the same time. Clutching to the random facts. Thinking the concept of a fact was itself a fiction. Because we live in a blur. All of us live in a blur.

I was starting to feel it again. Only this time no one was really watching.

12E

"What is the answer, Evan?" Ms. Granger asked.

Giraffe, I wanted to answer. It was on the tip of my tongue. *Giraffe*.

This was in math class.

12F

"Where is your homework?" Mr. McNulty asked.

~~*It's with Ariel.*~~

"There is no such thing as homework," I said.

"What?"

"I mean, I left it at home."

12G

If the photographer existed, I had to be able to find her.

~~But I couldn't find you, could I~~?

12H

You existed. You existed now as a fractal.

~~Definition:~~

~~A **fractal** is generally a rough or fragmented geometric shape that can be broken into parts, each of which is (at least approximately) a reduced-size copy of the whole.~~

Maybe I was a fractal. Maybe the photographer was a fractal. Maybe we were all fractals.

121

Matt was talking to me. For a moment I didn't recognize him.

"Are you okay?" he asked.

"I don't know what okay is," I said.

"What?"

"I mean . . . I don't know what *okay* means. No, not what it means. Where it comes from. Where does *okay* come from?"

We looked it up.

The answer: Nobody knows. They think it is a misspelled variation of *all correct*—either *oll korrect* or *ole kurreck*—but they're not really sure.

~~Meaning divorced from origin. And it's okay.~~

"Weird," Matt said.

"Yeah," I agreed.

He never noticed that I hadn't answered his first question.

12J

~~I wondered if this was how you'd felt.~~
~~I wondered if I was making myself feel how you'd felt.~~
~~I knew it wasn't a choice. It was just what my mind was doing.~~
~~Although I could've been fighting it more.~~

12K

~~*What if Jack is right? What if all these things that appear connected aren't really connected? What if none of us are connected?*~~

Then I opened my locker after school and found another photo waiting for me.

13

13A

On the back, someone—presumably the photographer—had written *4:00*.

Was that when the photo had been taken?

Or was that when I was supposed to be there?

I saw the skulls on her vest.

A coincidence?

A sign?

I had to find Jack, then find out.

13B

It was like the day hadn't happened. Or that it had only happened to me. He was out on the patio, talking to Miranda. She was laughing. He was smiling. They looked like they were ~~happy vulnerable flirting~~ together. It stopped me. In my mind, they were kissing, they had their hands all over each other. But then I blinked, and they were just standing there, talking. It was nothing. ~~I didn't want you to know about this.~~ I watched for another minute. They didn't do anything wrong. I knew I'd be interrupting, but that didn't seem wrong, either. Jack would want to know.

"Hey, Jack," I said, stepping close enough for him to hear, but not in their space yet. "Hey, Miranda."

"Hey," Miranda said.

"What's up, Ev?" Jack asked.

"Can I talk to you for a second?" I said, leaving the *alone* implied.

Miranda heard it.

"I'll just go get my stuff, okay?" she said. "Good to see you, Ev."

~~*You didn't even know my name*, I thought. *You're just repeating what he said.*~~

When she was gone, I took out the picture.

"It was in my locker. It has a time on the back. I think we're supposed to meet her or something. It's three now. We have an hour."

"Whoa, Evan. Just stop for a second."

~~I never said a bad word about him. The whole time the two of you were together. Not one bad thing.~~

"I know," I said. "It's a long stretch of railroad track. But I think she wants us to find her, so it's probably close by. And if you look in the back, there's a spot where the brown dirt turns into gray gravel, and there's also a kind of green post on the left side. We can look for those."

"Come on," Jack said. And I honestly thought we were setting off right away. But instead he was taking me to the ledge of the patio and sitting down. He patted the space next to him.

~~He was attractive. I knew that. And I knew that attractive people always got away with things. But I never said a bad word about him.~~

"I think we need to talk," he said.

~~Because he meant something to you. He did.~~

"Because I think you need to let this go."

"What?" I didn't understand.

"I said, I think you need to let this go."

~~He had been there.~~

~~With me.~~

~~He had been there with me.~~

"Not now!" I argued. "We're so close."

He shook his head. "I have something else I have to do."

"What?" I said. Then I pointed to the direction Miranda had walked off. "Her?"

"Not just her. Life, Evan. We have to go back to life. We have to let this go."

~~*"Let go!" she screamed. "Let go of me!"*~~

I wanted to cover my ears.

Jack went on. "I'm genuinely worried about you, Evan. Whoever's doing this with the photos is playing a sick joke on us, and you're falling for it. It's messed up and it has to stop. But it's not going to stop until we act like we don't care. It's not going to go away. We're not going to be able to move on."

"What?" I yelled back at him. "Do we just forget that she ever existed? Forget what happened?"

Jack shook his head. So sad. "No. That's not what I mean."

"Then what do you mean? *Letting go*. Do you really think it's there because we're holding on to it? Do you really think it's that easy? I'm not holding on to it, Jack. It's holding on to me. And it's holding on to you, whether you ignore it or not."

Jack's right hand curled into a fist. Not to hit me—just to be a fist.

"Look, Evan—I wasn't good at this with her, and I'm not good at it with you. I can't fight you over it. I can't. Call me whatever you want—*heartless* was a favorite of hers. And you know what, I'll have to take it. But I'd rather be called heartless than keep living in this mess she created. I thought it was going away, and now this evil girl is doing whatever she's doing with the photos and trying to pull it all back. But I can't play that game. It's a game, Evan. And sometimes you have to walk away. Don't play it."

"You're not heartless," I said. "She never called you heartless."

The fist unclenched, then went back to being a fist.

"Of course she did, Evan! I was there. There are times you have no idea about. You weren't always there. Just like I wasn't there when she was alone with you. She would disappear in front of me. And then she'd reappear and she'd say the most awful things—about me, about herself. Mostly about herself. Of course, now I know what it was, but I didn't know then. I was too caught by it. It hurt to hear those things, Evan. She would tear it all apart to find her 'truth.' If I tried to hold her, she'd tell me to get off. And if I just sat there, she'd say, 'Why aren't you holding me?' Long hours of this. And I'd be afraid to go, and I'd be afraid to stay. 'Just moods,' she'd finally say. 'I'm sorry—I was in a mood.' Well, yeah. That's what we both thought. That's what all of us thought, right? Because we didn't want to believe anything else."

"But, Jack—"

"No—let me finish. It's time we had this conversation. Because I don't think you've been angry at her yet—and you need to be angry at her. You think it's about what you didn't do and what I didn't do and maybe what her parents didn't do and what her other friends, whoever they were, didn't do. You might even think it's about what she didn't do. But mostly it's about what she *did*. Whether or not it was under her control, she did it. And if you've done any reading about it, you'll know that there isn't anything we could have done to stop it. It was inevitable. We were just lucky—or unlucky—enough to be there when all the pieces fell apart from each other."

~~A ***fractal*** *is generally a rough or fragmented geometric shape that can be broken into parts, each of which is (at least approximately) a reduced-size copy of the whole.*~~

"Evan, listen to me. I don't want you to fall apart, too. You understand? If this photographer shows up, I will gladly put her in her place. But you can't let it happen. And if you follow her, you're letting it happen. You are."

His voice was trying to be calm, but I could hear the fractures, I could feel him gluing the calmness together. I wanted to say *I need you*, but I figured you'd said that, too. I wanted to say *This has to be done*, but I knew it didn't have to be. Not to him. Because he was separating himself. And I couldn't.

"I'll go without you," I told him, gambling that he wouldn't let me go alone.

He tilted his head, disappointed. Then he slapped his hands on his thighs before standing up.

"You'll do what you're going to do," he said. "I'm not going to stop you. I just want you to realize that I tried. And that you can stop playing the game at any time. I can help you with that. But I can't help you play it. Not anymore."

"Is this because of Miranda?" I asked, not getting up.

"No," he said. "I had to let go of some of it before I could even talk to Miranda. I don't want you to think I got through this undamaged, okay? But I'm learning to live with it. Because otherwise, the damage is all you are."

Now I stood up.

"I'm going," I said.

"Fine," Jack said. "Just do me a favor. Whatever you find—don't let me know. Don't. I'm done."

I was still thinking he might come with me. Even after he left.

14

~~*Heartless. Heartless.*~~ *Heartless.*

You'd never called me that. Never.

~~But.~~

I was there for you. I was the one you trusted.

~~But.~~

I knew you.

~~*"You can't know me."*~~

I did.

~~*"You know one me. Just like I know one you. But you can't know every me, Evan. And I can't know every you."*~~

I didn't want this to be coming back. I didn't want to be having these conversations in my head.

~~*"It's not a conversation. You're the only one here."*~~

I wanted to find the spot on the train tracks. I was walking along the train tracks. Looking for that spot.

~~*"Fill your head with the right pictures of me. Fill your head with the ones you'd hang on a wall."*~~

Every now and then, a train would go by. But not too often. It wasn't rush hour yet.

~~"I'm still here. I'm just unreachable."~~

"Stop!" I yelled. "Just stop it!"

I knew Jack was right, but I also knew it didn't matter.

I had to see it through to the end. Because the end could be better. It couldn't be worse than this.

14A

3:30.

Walking.

3:45.

Blanking.

3:50.

Looking.

3:55.

There.

I didn't even have to see the change from dirt to gravel or the green post.

Because there they were.

Photographs. Taped lightly to the rails.

3:57.

I was within a hundred feet. And then I saw it.

The train.

Coming.

I ran.

Because the train would destroy the photographs.

I ran.

The noise of the train.

The first photo.

I shouldn't have taken the time to look. But I looked.

And then, written on the rail underneath:

I SAW

The second photo was four rails down.

I could feel the ground shaking.

The train coming.

I jumped over.

Underneath:

WHAT YOU DID

The train almost here.
The train.
The whistle.
The warning.
A screech.
The third photo.
The third.
In my fingers.

I could feel the train pushing the air.

Hear the howl.

I didn't look. I just read underneath—

TO HER

—and jumped to the side.

Hit **hard.**

The train screeching by.

I rolled on the gravel. Pieces of stone in my skin.

Crushing the photos as I rolled.

Imagining the people watching from the train.

The photographer watching.

I lost my breath.

~~*Deep breaths.*~~

I lifted myself up.

Blinking. Breathing.

~~*I wouldn't have died. I wouldn't have.*~~

Remembering the third photograph.

Looking at it there, on the side of the tracks, as the train pushed past.

Thinking: *WHO ARE YOU? WHO ARE YOU?*

~~*Aren't there any other clues?*~~

Hating life. You would say that all the time. *I hate life*. And I thought it was just something you said.

But I felt it. Down to my bones.

Linked to frustration.

I SAW

Linked to unfairness.

WHAT YOU

Linked to guilt.

DID

Linked to anger.

TO

Linked to helplessness.

HER.

Hate.

Hate.

Hate.

I dwelt within it as I walked home. I dwelt within it the whole night. The next morning.

Let it go, I imagined Jack saying. *Just let it go*.

And then I slipped the photos into his locker.

I wanted him to find them, too.

15

Do you remember the time the three of us got into a fight over Zeno's dichotomy paradox?

Jack hadn't known what it was, so you explained.

"It's about infinities and motion," you said. "I'm sure you've heard this. It's about how if you try to get to somewhere by halves, or any fraction, really, you will never actually get there, because ultimately there will be an infinitely small distance between you and your destination."

"The most common example is a wall," I chimed in. "That if I go halfway to the wall, then halfway of the halfway, then halfway of that, on and on, always halfway, I will never actually touch the wall."

"Isn't that sad?" you said. "I mean, isn't that really disturbing?"

"But why?" Jack said. "I don't get it."

"Because you'll never actually get there. You will spend your whole life making progress, but you'll never actually get there."

"Infinity is against us," I told him. "There's no way for us ever to count it or control it or understand it."

"Are you stoned?" Jack asked.

You didn't appreciate that.

"No," you said. "We're *thinking*. We're taking what we learn and we're applying it."

"But that makes no sense," Jack said.

"It makes perfect sense," you argued. "What about it doesn't make sense?"

"Well, duh, isn't the answer to never walk in half steps? I mean, putting aside the fact that it's physically impossible to walk forward, say, a thousandth of an inch, in order to be trapped in this paradox, you'd have to agree to its terms. And we don't have to do that. If you want to walk to the wall, you walk to the wall."

"But those are human terms," you said dismissively.

"Yeah, but aren't we human? Last time I checked, we were human."

You leaned into him then. Leaned in halfway. Then another halfway. Then another halfway. And kept slowly doing this until your lips were hovering over his, only a sliver of air away. You held there—until he pushed in and kissed you. You pulled away immediately, angry.

"Go to hell, Jack," you said. "Maybe there's more to the ~~Truth~~ truth than being human."

"Yeah," I said. "You might be human, Jack, but Ariel's mathematics. She's all mathematics."

~~*There are so many things I wish I hadn't said.*~~

15A

I thought he'd track me down. I thought he'd tell me right away about the photos he found in his locker. But instead it was Katie who tracked me down in study hall.

Katie could get away with things like walking into the library for study hall in a period when she didn't actually have study hall. She was pretty, and she was a good girl, and thus the librarian didn't need to see a pass from her. If she was here, there had to be a reason for her to be here. There was no way that Katie would disrupt the universe by being somewhere she wasn't supposed to be.

We were friends, mostly because we'd grown up together. I liked her, and had good memories with her, but I wouldn't have said she meant all that much to me. At least not until that moment.

She looked around the library first. Then, when she saw me alone at my table, she came straight over. I was staring in her direction, half in my scatterthoughts, half out, so I noticed her coming over without really making a move to acknowledge it.

"I have something for you," she said, reaching into one of her textbooks. She was wearing dangling earrings, and I leaned to the left so they would bounce a little light my way.

"Here," she said, putting a photo on the desk.

"Where did you get that?" I asked. I couldn't imagine Katie hanging out with a guy with a Mohawk. But for a second—a split second—I thought, *Maybe it's her.* After all, she had a camera. She could've just asked some other girl to stand in for her, to throw me off. ~~Or maybe you had somehow gotten to her. Maybe you were behind it all.~~

Katie sat down across from me.

"I knew you'd ask me that," she said. "So here's the thing—if you want me to tell you where I got it, you're going to have to tell me why you need it."

~~I didn't trust her.~~ She pushed her bangs behind her right ear and looked at me. ~~I had to trust her.~~ Waiting for an answer.

~~I thought: *Ariel said you were one of the last girls to stop sleeping with her stuffed animals. She said you cared more about boys than girls. She said she missed you, but then she said she didn't understand why.*~~

"Somebody's been leaving photos for me," I said. "In my locker. Around. Whoever took this photo—she's leaving photos for me."

Katie tilted her head. "But why?"

"I don't know why. ~~If I knew why, do you think I'd be getting other people involved?~~"

"You've got to have an idea. . . ."

"I think it has to do with Ariel."

This was the thing: None of us talked about you. Not months later. Not now.

For a moment, during her pause, my mind ran away and I was picturing Katie twenty years older, as an adult. Like we were sitting at some airport bar and had just seen each other for the first time in years. This was still what we were talking about. And then you were coming over to our table. You, older. But I couldn't tell which one of us you were walking toward. ~~Or if you were a ghost.~~

"What do you mean, it has to do with Ariel?" Katie asked.

"Some of the pictures are of Ariel. The photographer knew

her. But I don't know the photographer." I matched Katie's glance. "Unless I do."

Katie shook her head. "It's not me. But when you showed us that photo at lunch, it made me think of something. . . ."

"Where did you find the photo?"

Katie lowered her voice, as if this, of all the things that had just been said, was the biggest secret.

"It was submitted to the literary magazine," she murmured. "About a week ago."

I was close. So close.

"Who submitted it?" I asked, trying to remain calm.

"I don't know. Submissions are anonymous."

"What do you mean, submissions are anonymous? Someone must know who submits things."

Katie leaned back. "Yeah, Mr. Rogers. But he keeps the list under lock and key."

~~So close, but still not touching the wall.~~

I wanted to hit the table so hard that my hand would split all of its atoms. I wanted to cause breakage and explosions.

I slumped down in my chair, and Katie sat up, her whole body now dangling over me.

"Evan," she said, "why do you always have to be so alone?"

I would have expected you to say this, or Fiona, or maybe even Jack, if he were angry. Not Katie.

"What do you mean?" I asked.

"Even after Ariel left us . . . you just wrapped yourself up in your pain, and the rest of us were all outside of it. I'm not saying you had no reason to be in pain—I'm not saying I was anywhere near as close to her as you were. But still. It's like you and Jack have the monopoly on it, you know."

"You thought she was a downer," I reminded her.

Katie actually laughed at that. "She *was* a downer, some of the time. Hell, I'd even say most of the time. But there are things you don't know, Evan."

"Like what?" I tried to make it not sound like a challenge, but it was one, and it ended up sounding that way.

"I'm going to guess that you haven't spent a lot of time in the girls' room—have you?"

Did she really want me to answer?

"Well, you'd be surprised how much time Ariel spent in the girls' room. Second floor, foreign language wing was her favorite, but she could also be found in first floor, math wing, and first floor, right off the gym. Not smoking. Not throwing up. Not doing what you usually do in there. No, she'd just be sitting in the stall. Sometimes with her music on, sometimes all quiet.

"We'd ask her what was wrong, and sometimes she'd answer, and sometimes she wouldn't. Fiona tried real hard—we both did. One day I couldn't take it anymore—it was obvious that she was just sitting there, and the locks are really easy to open from the outside, so I just let myself into her stall and closed the door again behind me. She wasn't crying or anything—I could've dealt with crying. Instead she looked like she was arguing with herself. You could tell. And I told her she needed to get help. Like, serious help. I used to go to a therapist for some messed-up family things, and I told her I could go with her, or we could find someone else. But she said no. She didn't get all into it—she didn't try to defend herself or tell me there wasn't anything wrong. She just said no. Then 'Sorry, no.' And that was it. I stood there, wanting something more. But she went back to wherever she was, and it was awkward to stay standing there, watching her. So I let myself out. And she stayed in there until after I left.

"That was the week before, Evan. It's not like she didn't know her options. She knew them. But she said no. *Sorry, no.*"

The week before. ~~"The things you love are the things that will destroy you," you'd said. And why hadn't I heard? Was I so used to you making these pronouncements?~~

"She wanted help," I found myself saying to Katie. ~~Didn't you? ANSWER ME. *Didn't you?*~~ "In the end. She wanted help."

Katie took my hand in hers. "I know," she said. "Which is why you did the right thing."

I forced myself not to pull away, not to pull my hand back, not to run.

~~*You don't know what you're talking about.*~~

Holding Katie's hand felt like betraying you, although I wasn't sure why. I wasn't even sure why betraying you was something that mattered anymore.

"I'll help you find the photographer," Katie said. "If only so we can tell him or her to stop."

"I'm pretty sure it's a her," I said. If I hadn't left the photos in Jack's locker, I could've shown them to her.

Katie didn't ask why. She just nodded and said, "Well, I'm going to tell Mr. Rogers I lost the photo, and when he takes out the list to see whose it is, I'm going to look over his shoulder. Or something like that. It shouldn't take long."

"Okay."

"And, Evan, if you ever want to talk . . . I don't always have to push my way into it."

It was a joke, but there was an unintentional echo in the joke:

Hadn't she pretty much told you the same thing?

16

Why wasn't Jack talking to me? I looked for him during school, then after school, but I didn't see him.

I went home and did my homework. I remembered how I used to define these times by the fact that I wasn't with you—you were out with Jack, or doing something else. It didn't even matter what it was, only that it wasn't with me. And when we were together, I was at home in the universe.

~~Or was that just the way it seemed now?~~

I wondered if I should get help. I wondered if this was how you felt. I wondered if I was just trying to make myself feel what you felt. I wondered if you were somehow rewiring my mind.

No. I wasn't wondering if you were somehow rewiring my mind. ~~That was the kind of thing you would have said.~~

Zeros and ones. I willed my mind back to zeros and ones.

16A

At ten, Katie emailed. She hadn't been able to talk to Mr. Rogers. She promised she'd try tomorrow.

16B

At eleven, Jack still hadn't emailed or anything.

16C

At midnight—precisely at midnight—I received a new email. It was from someone calling herself avengingariel.

you won't get away with it.
I will haunt you forever.

There was an attachment. When I opened it, you filled the screen.

16D

16E

You were looking right at me.

I broke.

~~Ariel, what did I do to you? What do you think I did to you? I always thought you were the strong one. I thought you could take anything. When you talked about the Truth, I thought you knew something that I didn't. I was just following. I didn't realize how bad it was. And then, when I saw how bad it was, I did the only thing I could do. You wanted help, didn't you? But in a moment, you went from being grateful to being so angry. And that anger is what I'm left with. Because it makes me doubt, Ariel. It makes me doubt everything. And I wish you were here, because you're the only one who can tell me what to do. Are you sending these photographs? Is this from you? Because I'm starting to understand. Really, I am. How maddening the Truth must have been. To think it's out there, and to know you can't get to it. We only see representations, not the real Truth. Was that what was wrong? Did that take over who you were? Ariel, you have to stop this. Ariel, I can't take this. Ariel, all I ever did was love you. And if it didn't work, I'm sorry. It was all I could do. You left me~~

~~with no choice. YOU LEFT ME WITH NO CHOICE. Does that make sense to you, Ariel? Can you make sense anymore? Is sense any different from the Truth? I know it is. I know it is. You would tell me how unhappy you were, but I thought you meant at that moment. I didn't realize how it fills you. Did it fill you, Ariel? Or is *happiness* another of the fake words? Ariel, I'm trying to understand. Ariel, you won't go away. I couldn't want you to go away even if it meant surviving. No. I want you to go away. I want this to stop. I miss you so much. Ariel, I know you can't hear this. Are you listening?~~

I pressed my head into my pillow and I screamed. Pure sound. No words. But it all came out as your name to me.

My mother came running into my room.

"What's wrong?" she asked. Then, again, "Evan? What's wrong?"

She saw the photo on my computer.

"Oh, Evan," she said. "Please."

She tried. Everyone tried with me. And every time, it felt like the whole point of life was to see if trying was ever enough.

17

At five in the morning, there was another email from avengingariel. I wasn't awake then, but I got it when I checked before school.

> **you were never worthy of her.**
> **she knew so much more than you did.**
> **so you had to destroy her.**
> **you think you saved her. but you destroyed her.**

17A

17B

I gave up almost immediately. It was a field. With some trees. Maybe a building. I zoomed in, but it all blurred. And part of me didn't even care. It all seemed pointless. ~~*Pointless . . . without point . . . round . . . full circle.*~~

I packed up to go to school.

I forwarded the email to Jack before I went.

17C

Katie found me before homeroom and pulled me into an empty classroom to talk.

"Mr. Rogers is out today," she said. "I couldn't stand it, so I . . . well, I went through his desk. I didn't find the list, though. He must keep it with him, or at home or something. I even tried looking on his computer. I'm so glad I wasn't caught."

There was a thrill in Katie's voice as she told me all this. ~~It reminded me a little of you. Or of me when I was around you.~~

"I guess we'll have to wait until Monday," Katie said.

I couldn't imagine waiting that long.

17D

I thought I saw her in the hallway.

It was between classes. Crowded.

But I tried. I pushed

through the conversations

pushed

past the bystanders

pushed

even though some people pushed back, told me to watch it.

She was ahead of me. I swore it.

But I was losing sight of her.

Instead I saw Mrs. McGuinness coming out of the guidance office.

~~*"It wasn't your fault, Evan! You did the right thing!"*~~

Mrs. McGuinness, noticing me.

~~*"She was sick! If she'd been bleeding on the street, you would've run to get help. It's the same thing!"*~~

Mrs. McGuinness, realizing it had been a while since one of our chats.

~~*"I'm here for you, Evan! We're all here for you!"*~~

I had to stop pushing. I had to turn around. I couldn't let her talk to me.

17E

You hated her so much.

"They're so far from the Truth," you'd say. "Guidance? Is that what they call it. Guidance toward what? Interesting how they never specify that."

"If she'd been bleeding on the street, you would've run to get help. It's the same thing!"

"Typical," I could hear you saying back. "The whole point is that I wasn't bleeding in the street. I wasn't dying of cancer. You couldn't take an X-ray and see what was wrong with me. You couldn't make such an easy diagnosis. You had to guess. And everybody guessed wrong."

But the thing is, I hadn't even made the guess. I trusted that you knew what you were doing.

You were very convincing.

And I destroyed you.

17F

I hadn't even gotten my lunch before Jack pulled me away from it.

"Let's take a walk," he said, gesturing me out of the lunch line.

"~~Am I in trouble~~? What's going on?" I asked.

But he waited until we were out back. I thought we'd stay on the patio, but we walked even farther away, beyond all the sound waves from the school.

"I got your email this morning," he said. He didn't look too happy about it. "I can't believe this girl, whoever she is, would do that to you. Is this the first time she's emailed?"

I shook my head. "There was one other. A picture of Ariel."

Jack went for a cigarette from his pocket, but came up short.

"Left them in my locker." He looked at me. "And I'm pretty sure you don't have one."

"You are correct," I said.

~~"*You are correct.*" That was something you used to say, and we both knew it. I had gotten that from you.~~

"Look," he went on, "I talked to Miranda about this. Last

night, even before I got your email. I didn't tell her everything—she doesn't need to know everything about Ariel and what happened. But I told her about the photos. And you know what she said? She said, 'That girl is stalking you and Evan. It's stalking.' I guess I knew that, but having her say it made me realize how wrong it was. And you know what? We've only been encouraging her by playing along. I know I told you this last time, but now I really mean it—we have to walk away. Or, if you don't want to think of it as walking away, we have to make her a little scared. Even if you know where the field is in that picture, don't go there. Stay away. I doubt that will be the last we'll hear from her. But we'll get to see what she does when we don't play along."

I knew it wasn't the point, but I said, "You told Miranda?"

We'd reached the bleachers for the football field. There were a couple of people running on the track, but otherwise it was empty. Jack walked up to the top row and sat down. I followed.

Every you, every me. I wondered if Jack was a different Jack with Miranda. I wondered if we all just kept changing, or splitting off. I wondered if I didn't meet anyone new, if I didn't talk to anyone else, would I stay the same me?

"What are you thinking, Evan?"

So I told him.

Every you, every me. Fractals. Fractures.

"I wonder who she is now," I said.

"So do I," Jack admitted. "All the time."

18

I promised Jack I wouldn't find the field from the photo. I promised him I wouldn't go there. I promised him to give the photographer nothing but silence.

And this time, I actually kept my promise.

18A

I was talking to you more and more. Remembering times that weren't complicated. Asking you how you were. Begging for forgiveness, if only so you'd say it wasn't necessary.

You never said anything back.

18B

do you really think you can ignore me?
if so, then you don't know me.
the same way you don't know her.
you think she was weak, but I know she was brave.
I understood. you didn't.
I still understand. you don't.

18C

Avengingariel must have gone to the field. She must have waited.

I wondered if this photo was from the same field, only from a different angle. Clearer. With a better landmark.

I wondered if *avenging* was being used as an adjective or a verb.

I forwarded the email to Jack, this time with a message:

I'm not going.

He sent an email back:

Good.

18D

My parents wanted to take a drive on Saturday. I said okay.

My mother said I should have a "change of scenery." The word *scenery* made me think of a play. And as we were driving around, it made sense that way. Because no matter how much the scenery changed, we were still on the same stage.

Your life is inescapable. ~~Unless you decide to escape it.~~

My parents asked about school. About friends. About colleges. About what I was reading. And as I sat there, I felt again like you. Your parents must have asked you the same questions. They must have tried the same way. Knowing there was a problem, but thinking it would be a bigger problem if they brought it up. So instead they tried to muffle it with ordinary things. They saw the scenery, not the stage.

~~*"So it's all come full circle," you said.*~~

"Would you like that?" my mother asked.

"What?" I said.

"To go rafting over the summer. To go away."

~~"Let's talk about the summer like it's sure to exist," you whispered in my ear. This wasn't a memory. You were whispering it~~

~~now. "But you and I know better, don't we? How about we do away with the summer?"~~

"That sounds great," I said.

18E

I imagined the photographer in that field. Waiting for me.

I knew it was right to avoid her. I knew we had to pretend like we were ignoring her, like she wasn't having any effect.

But I pictured her there, waiting. And I knew: She had something to say to me. Something I didn't want to hear. But something that I would hear eventually, whether I wanted to or not.

Why else do this?

Why else try to pen us in?

She had something to say.

~~You had something to say.~~

It felt good to imagine ~~you~~ her waiting. It felt good to imagine how ~~you~~ she felt when the sun set and I wasn't there. It felt good to imagine ~~your~~ her next photograph in the middle of that field, eventually blowing away.

But the good feeling, like the avoidance, was only temporary.

I knew we were simply postponing the inevitable.

The only difference this time was that at least we could see it coming.

18F

When we got home from the drive, after having dinner in town, I went straight to my room. I wanted to call Jack, but then I realized he was probably out at some party with the team. The first month or so, he'd invited me along. But I couldn't picture myself there, numb to everyone else. So I let him go. And he stopped asking, after a while.

I heard my mother open the front door, open the mailbox, come back inside. The usual pattern of coming home, as normal as my father turning on the television.

Only this time she called out my name. Then she walked upstairs. Stood in my doorway.

"There was something for you in the mailbox," she said. Curious, but not curious enough to say more.

She handed me an envelope with my name written on it.

I didn't move to open it until she was gone, until I could close the door.

19

Another photo of me.
Another photo of that day.

~~*"Let's go into the woods and take some pictures," you said. "I found this old camera."*~~

~~*"Sure," I said. "After school?"*~~

~~*"Yeah, after school."*~~

~~*And what happened during school? What changed?*~~

~~*Because when I met you at your locker, you were different. You handed me the camera.*~~

~~*"Here, take this."*~~

~~*But you were distracted.*~~

~~*"What's wrong?" I asked.*~~

~~And—yes, I remember.~~
~~You said, "Everything."~~

~~I followed you into the woods.~~
~~I followed you.~~
~~I would have followed you anywhere.~~
~~I thought that.~~
~~And then you went somewhere I couldn't follow.~~

~~*But back up. Return to the woods. Look at the picture. There you are. Someone was watching. I have no idea who. But there I am.*~~

~~*I must be looking at you.*~~

~~*You didn't take this photo.*~~

~~*I had the camera.*~~

~~*"Take my picture," you said.*~~

~~*So I lined up the old camera.*~~

~~*"Is there film in this?" I asked.*~~

~~*"This way, you'll have me for posterity," you said.*~~

~~*"What do you mean?" I asked. I wasn't sure there was any film.*~~

~~*"Evan, I can't take it right now. I just can't take it."*~~

~~*"Take what?"*~~

~~*"Take the picture."*~~

~~*"What?"*~~

~~*"I said, take the picture."*~~

~~*What happened next?*~~

~~*What happened next was*~~

~~*What happened next was*~~

~~*Jack?*~~

~~*No.*~~

~~*Yes.*~~

~~*Your scream.*~~

~~*No.*~~

~~*Yes.*~~

~~*What happened next.*~~

~~*Stop.*~~

~~*What happened*~~

~~*Stop.*~~

~~Next~~

~~*"Stop!"*~~

~~*Stop.*~~

I was tearing up the photograph.

I couldn't stop tearing up the photograph.

I was telling myself to stop.

I was hearing you yell. ~~*"Stop!"*~~
I cannot stop it.

~~*I cannot stop it.*~~

20

I wore myself out and slept most of Sunday. On Monday, school was a full hive when I got there. I ran to the patio, hoping to find ~~you~~ Jack. Sure enough, there he was, and it even looked like he was waiting for me. When he saw me, he put out his cigarette and said something to Katie, who was standing next to him. They both came over, heading me off before I got over to where they'd been.

"Hey," I said. "Something happened."

Something was wrong. I could tell. Jack was looking at me strangely. Like *I* had done something wrong. Really wrong.

"Let's talk over there," he said, gesturing a little ways off, into the woods.

"I got another photo," I told him. Katie, I noticed, wouldn't look me in the eye.

"Of course you did," he said.

"What?"

But he wouldn't answer. Not until we were away from everyone else, in the trees. And even then, he only stared at me. It was Katie who broke the silence.

"I caught Mr. Rogers this morning," she said. "He's back in school."

That's it, I thought. *They've found the girl.*

"Who is she?" I asked.

"I told him I needed to contact the person who took the photo. I told him I'd damaged it and needed another print."

"And?"

"He yelled at me for being careless. But then he gave me the name and told me to be more careful next time."

Now she stopped.

I couldn't stand it.

"Who is she?" I asked again.

Katie shook her head.

And Jack said, "It's you."

~~*It's you It's you It's you*~~

"What?" ~~*I don't understand.*~~

Now Jack was grabbing my shirt. Pushing me against a tree. Katie telling him to stop. But he was knocking me back. It hurt, but it didn't hurt so much, because part of me wasn't even there.

"I said, it's you, Evan. The person who submitted that photo is YOU."

"But it can't be!" ~~*it can't be it can't be*~~

"Stop lying!"

He knocked my head back. *Pain.*

"Did you think we wouldn't find out?"

~~*it can't be it can't be*~~

"It wasn't me," I said.

He shoved me. Hard. I bent over.

"Jack—stop!" Katie was yelling at him now.

~~*"Stop!"*~~

He didn't pay any attention to her, hovering over me, shouting. "So is Mr. Rogers lying? Is that what you're saying?"

"It wasn't me! She must have put my name on it. She's after us, Jack!"

"Ah, yes, the mysterious 'she.' Only thing is, she doesn't exist."

Now Katie was in between us. Shielding me.

"Jack, stop."

He pulled back for a moment, took something out of his back pocket, and threw it at the ground in front of me.

"Are you saying you didn't leave this in my locker this morning?"

~~*I didn't I didn't*~~ I shook my head.

"Evan, what are you doing?"

I was shivering. Shaking.

"I'm not doing anything." ~~*I'm in the photos.*~~ "Look—how can I have taken the photos? I'm in them."

"Well, maybe she took them."

And I knew which *she* he meant. Not the mystery girl.

You.

I could barely look at him.

"You think we did this together?" I asked.

"*Jack,*" Katie cautioned.

He wouldn't relent. "I think you're just as bad as she is. No—maybe even worse. Because she took it all out on herself. You're taking it out on other people. That's definitely worse.

"I don't know what I did to you to make you do this, Evan. Is it jealousy? Did you want to be the boyfriend? Did you hate that you couldn't have her all to yourself? I'd almost understand that. But why now, Evan? Why bring it all up now? Does it really kill you so bad that I'm not miserable and pathetic like you? Is it really so bad that I'm getting over it and you're not?"

"I didn't do it."

"And what about the other ones you put in my locker? I saw you that morning. How do you explain that?"

"I wanted you to see them. She left them on the train tracks and I—"

"Oh, yeah—you didn't want me missing out. Maybe I'm the pathetic one, because I actually believed that."

~~*It's not me. It's not. It's not.*~~

"Evan," Katie said, calmer. "We just want to know why you did it."

~~*"No one believes me," you said. "No one ever believes me."*~~

Jack leaned down again to me. I tried to look away, but he grabbed my chin, forced me to look at him.

~~*I don't want to be the center of attention.*~~

"You might think you were doing some kind of revenge," he said, "but let me tell you—she would hate you for it. She never would have done this to any of us. Even at her worst."

~~*I don't want to be the center of anything.*~~

The second bell rang, marking the start of homeroom. I stayed slumped against the tree, pain radiating throughout my body.

"I'm through with you," Jack said. "Do you understand? Completely through."

I nodded, but he wasn't even looking. He was already walking away.

"You need help," Katie said, and the tone of her voice made it unclear whether or not she was offering it herself.

"I didn't do it," I said. "That's what she wants you to think."

"She's gone, Evan."

But I wasn't talking about you.

I was talking about your avenger.

20A

I had to find her. My only way out was to find her.

20B

~~*It's you. You deserve this. There is a reason this is happening to you.*~~

20C

I didn't go to homeroom. I didn't go to class.
I walked through the halls.
Looking for her.

20D

~~"You're not going to find me,"~~ you said. ~~"You'll never find me."~~

~~No. Not *said*. Not past tense.~~

~~You were saying it now.~~

20E

If she submitted that photo to the literary magazine as a way of trapping me If she broke into my locker If she could follow me so closely . . . she had to be somewhere in this school.

~~*if if if if*~~

~~*"Only thing is, she doesn't exist."*~~

~~*Stop it, Jack. You don't know.*~~

20F

During first period, I went to my own locker.

There was something waiting for me.

"Who are you?" I screamed. ~~*are you doing this to me?* **WHY** *are you doing this to me?*~~

There was no ~~response~~ note, no time to meet her, no hint at where to go.

20G

~~If it had been you, people would have noticed. People would all be talking about you coming back.~~

20H

I checked my email.

this is it.
this is what it feels like to be helpless.

201

I peered into every classroom. I didn't care which teachers saw me.

~~*You deserve this. You deserve this. You deserve this.*~~

~~*"Take my picture," you said.*~~

~~*So I lined up the old camera.*~~

~~*"Is there film in this?" I asked.*~~

Fiona found me between third and fourth periods.

"What's going on?" she asked.

"Nothing," I said. How could I begin to tell her?

"Evan—" She put her hand on my shoulder. Or tried to.

I ducked away. "It's nothing, Fiona."

~~*I am not the center of attention.*~~

"You can't . . ."

"What, Fiona? What can't I do?"

"You can't do this alone."

"You know what?" I said. "I've been doing it alone ever since they took Ariel away."

~~away gone exiled over~~

"What do you mean?" Fiona asked, too much concern in her voice. I couldn't take it.

"I don't have to explain!" I shouted, pulling away from her.

~~*I am not the center of anything.*~~

20J

The avenger had to eat lunch, and since there was only one hallway leading to the cafeteria, I stationed myself there for all the lunch periods. She had been at school this morning to put the photo in Jack's locker. She had to be here now.

People noticed me sitting in the hallway. I had a book open, to pretend to be studying. But really I was studying them. All the patterns that you found incomprehensible. All the patterns that overwhelmed you. You thought they spelled the Truth. And I'd believed you, ~~far longer than I should have~~.

Red shirt. Blue shirt. White shirt. Black shirt.

First lunch period came: nothing.

Blue shirt. White shirt. Black shirt. Black shirt. Blue shirt.

Second lunch period came: When I saw Jack, Katie, and Fiona, I looked down, hoped they didn't see me. The only person who said hello was Charlie, and I figured Katie hadn't told him anything.

Pink shirt. White shirt. Yellow and green stripes. Black shirt. Black shirt.

Third lunch period. I was hungry. This was my last chance,

and I hadn't seen her yet. Still, I had to eat. I went into the cafeteria and it was so strange—I'd always had second lunch, so it was like they had taken all the people I knew from the cafeteria and switched them with strangers. All the wrong faces were at all the right tables. I scanned around, acting like I was looking for a place to sit, but really looking for her.

Nothing. Nothing. Nothing.

I know she exists. Like I exist. Like Ariel exists somewhere.

Nothing.

Nothing.

I finished my lunch.

Nothing.

Put my tray away.

Nothing.

Nothing.

Went back into the hallway.

Looked at all the people leaving.

Nothing.

Nothing.

And then

21

There she was.

It had to be her.

21A

She was walking alone. But there were too many people around. I couldn't just stop her with all these people around.

I was sure it was her.

It had to be her.

I followed her away from the cafeteria. To her locker, in a corridor far from mine, far from Jack's. She put down her backpack. She was spinning the combination.

I didn't know what I was going to say. I walked right up to her. She turned to look at me.

It was her. It had to be her.

"It's you," I said.

"Excuse me?" she replied. She didn't look exactly the same, but she looked the same enough. She was chewing gum. She didn't seem to know me.

"You're the one who's been sending us the photos," I said.

She looked at me like she didn't know what I was talking about.

"I think you have the wrong girl," she said. She opened her locker.

"Why are you doing it?" I asked.

She looked back at me, annoyed.

"Doing what?"

"The photos."

"*What* photos?"

~~*She doesn't know.*~~

~~*She knows.*~~

"Stop it," I said. "I know who you are."

~~*It has to be her.*~~

"Look, freak," she said, getting mad now, "I have to go to class. I think you've mistaken me for someone else. Because I have no idea what you're saying."

~~*It's her, right?*~~

"Ariel," I said.

She shook her head. "I'm afraid I'm not Ariel. Sorry."

She was taking a book from her locker. She was closing the locker. She was going to go. She was going to vanish again.

"No—stop," I said.

~~*It has to be her.*~~

"Are you crazy?"

~~*A girl in the cafeteria. "You must be crazy, too."*~~

I didn't know what I was doing. But I felt I needed to do it.

I grabbed her backpack and started to run.

22

"Hey!" she yelled.

I ran.

~~*"I don't need your help!" you screamed.*~~

I ran.

~~*"You're against me! Both of you—you're against me."*~~

I passed Jack and Katie talking in the hall.

~~*"I'll kill myself. I swear, I'll kill myself," you threatened.*~~

I was sure she was running after me.

~~*"We're not going to leave you alone," I said.*~~

She had to be running after me.

~~*I am not the center of anything.*~~

I imagined all the cameras taking pictures of me. Capturing me as I ran. Capturing me, but not catching me.

I imagined her behind the camera, smiling.

Out of the school.

Out into the air.

~~*"That's the question, isn't it?" you said one night. "Does death bring freedom, or is it the end of freedom?"*~~

Right into the woods.

Farther.

Farther.

Back to where it happened.

Back.

Back.

Hearing them behind me.

Running out of breath.

Knowing this had to be the place.

~~*I followed you into the woods.*~~

~~*I followed you.*~~

~~*I would have followed you anywhere.*~~

~~*I thought that.*~~

~~*And then you went somewhere I couldn't follow.*~~

They followed me.

~~*"Here," you said.*~~

~~*"Take my picture," you said.*~~

"What are you *doing*, Evan?" Jack was yelling.

"It's her," I said, pointing to the girl. "Can't you see it's her?"

"I'm so sorry," Katie was saying to her.

~~*"I'm so sorry," I cried to you. And the way you looked at me, I knew I was never going to see you again.*~~

"He has my bag," she said.

"Evan, give her back her bag," Jack ordered.

~~*"Evan, get help. I'll stay here. You get help."*~~

~~*"You need help," Katie said.*~~

I pulled at the zipper.

I opened the bag.

~~*It has to be her.*~~

I turned it upside down.

I turned all our lives over.

22A

Notebooks.
Mechanical pencils.
Film.
Assignments.
And there.
At the bottom.
Now at the top.
You.

22B

22C

We froze.

For a second, we were all stilled by the sight of you.

Then I picked up the photo.

"You put that in there," the girl said. She turned to Katie and Jack. "He put that in there."

"I don't know what to believe," Jack said.

I looked at one of her assignments. Looked at the top.

"Dana," I said. "Your name is Dana."

"This is insane," she said. "You can't just steal my things. I'm going to get the principal."

She turned to go.

Katie blocked her.

"Sorry," Katie said, "but . . . I don't think you're going anywhere yet."

Dana turned back to me. Made a decision. Stalked over and grabbed the photo out of my hand.

"You don't deserve this," she said. "None of you ever deserved her."

Before I could say something else, she went on. "Didn't you

ever ask whose camera it was, Evan? Didn't you ever wonder? You knew it wasn't hers."

~~*"Let's go into the woods and take some pictures," you said. "I found this old camera."*~~

"What camera?" Jack asked. "What is she talking about?"

~~*How is it that this can hurt me the most? The piece I never knew. The piece you never told me.*~~

"She was there," I explained. "She was watching."

~~*Why didn't you ever say? Why didn't you tell us?*~~

"It was my camera," she said. "And afterwards, when I wanted it back, her parents gave it to me."

~~*Your parents knew her.*~~

"Who *are* you?" Jack asked.

"I'm her best friend," she said. "Ariel's best friend."

"No," I said.

~~Maybe relationships could have fractals, too. And maybe that sense of loss was when you're becoming a fractal of what you once were to each other.~~

~~*Best friend.* Who set up that phrase? Who made it a competition?~~

~~Those nights. The ones when you weren't with us. I guess you were with her.~~

"Yes. We hung out all the time. Took pictures together. She even flirted with my cousin when he came to visit. You know him—I think you've sent him emails. Alex?"

~~*All this time. All this time.*~~

"She didn't—" Jack said.

"How do you know what she did or didn't do? You didn't

even know I existed, did you?" She actually smiled at that. "Our little secret. I loved that."

~~*"Our little secret." You used to tell me that all the time. Something we kept from your parents. Or something we kept from Jack. Or something we kept from the world.*~~

"You have no idea what you're talking about," Jack said.

But she did. She had more than an idea. I could see that. It was there in her voice. That knowledge of you. That knowledge.

She turned on him ~~with an echo of your indignation~~. "I know *exactly* what I'm talking about. Were you with her all the time, Jack? Did you know everything about her? I'm walking proof that you didn't. But she'd tell me about you, Jack. Where you had your first kiss—did you like that part, Jack? Where you'd go. What you'd do. How you didn't understand what she was going through. She told me because I *did* understand what she was going through. We would hang out, mostly at night. We'd just wander around, and she'd tell me all of her dark things and I'd tell her mine. She saw things neither of you could see. I guess that scared you. But it didn't scare me. And in the end, I was the only one who didn't betray her. You guys did that."

And there it was.

Right there.

"You *really* have no idea what you're talking about," Jack said.

"I saw you do it. I saw you destroy her."

"We saved her," I said.

Dana looked at me like I was the biggest fool in the world.

"No," she said. "You destroyed her. She wanted to die, and you didn't let her."

"How can you say that?" Katie asked. "That's ridiculous."

~~*"Take my picture," you said.*~~

~~*So I lined up the old camera.*~~

~~*"Is there film in this?" I asked.*~~

~~*"This way, you'll have me for posterity," you said.*~~

"She was supposed to go out with me. I'd given her my camera. Then I couldn't do it, and she asked you guys. Or at least you, Evan. I ended up being free, so when the time came, I followed you. With my real camera. I thought she'd get a kick out of that—me taking pictures of her taking pictures. We did that all the time with each other. But she never got to take a picture that day, did she? You guys had other plans."

"It wasn't planned," I said.

"Maybe not for you. For her, I think it was. It was a test. And you failed."

"Shut up," Jack said.

She shook her head. "Too late. You can't shut either of us up, no matter how hard you try."

"How could you have watched?" I asked. "How could you have just stood there and watched?"

~~*"What do you mean?" I asked. I wasn't sure there was any film.*~~

~~*"Evan, I can't take it right now. I just can't take it."*~~

~~*"Take what?"*~~

~~*"Take the picture."*~~

~~*"What?"*~~

~~*"I said, take the picture."*~~

"What was I going to do?" Dana shot back. "There was no way to free her. You always wanted to clip her wings. And then you did it. All of you."

~~*But I put the camera down.*~~

~~*"Tell me," I said.*~~

~~*"I want a gun, Evan. I'm telling you, I want a gun."*~~

"How can you say that?" Jack yelled. "We weren't destroying her. She was destroying herself."

~~*"I'm not getting you a gun," I said, knowing it wasn't a joke.*~~

~~*"It won't even matter whether you do or not. I can't take it anymore."*~~

~~*"Stop it," I said.*~~

~~*"I can't." You were starting to cry. "I just can't."*~~

~~*And then you started screaming.*~~

"You're crazy," Jack said to her.

"Oh, is that right?" Dana said. "Just like *she* was crazy. I'll bet you told her that all the time."

"No," I said.

"No?"

"No. Because we didn't see it until it was too late."

~~*I couldn't make you stop.*~~

~~*I called Jack.*~~

~~*"You have to help me," I said to him. "We have to help her."*~~

~~*You wouldn't let me near you. You wouldn't let me touch you. You were ripping at yourself. You were trying to tear yourself apart.*~~

"She isn't crazy," Dana said. "She sees through all the phoniness. She sees what the world is really like. And the world can't stand girls like that. The world has to put them in their place, put them away. You wanted her to be this uncomplicated girl, but by trying to force her to be that girl, you unraveled her."

~~*When Jack got there, he didn't even ask me what was going on.*~~

~~*He went right to you. Grabbed you. Tried to ground you. And you slapped him. Slapped him slapped him slapped him.*~~

"She was *psychotic*!" Jack yelled. "She was in the middle of a breakdown!"

~~*"Evan, get help. I'll stay here. You get help."*~~

~~*But I wanted to be the one to stay.*~~

"You took away her right to be herself," Dana yelled back. "When she was with me, she wasn't like that."

~~*"I don't need your help!" you screamed.*~~

~~*"Yes, you do," he told you. "Evan and I both think that."*~~

~~*"You're against me! Both of you—you're against me."*~~

"Don't you wonder why she doesn't want to see you?"

~~*"That's not it," I said. "That's not it at all." But I wasn't sure you could hear me over your crying.*~~

"Don't you wonder why she hates you?"

~~*"They'll be here soon," Jack said. "It's for the best."*~~

~~*I was glad he sounded so confident. Because I was starting to wonder whether we'd done the right thing.*~~

~~*"I'll kill myself. I swear, I'll kill myself," you threatened.*~~

~~*"We're not going to leave you alone," I said.*~~

"Don't you feel guilty about what you've done?"

~~*But then I did leave. I had to leave. Because I couldn't find your phone. I didn't know how to reach your mother. So I ran. I ran to your house. I pounded on the door. And when your mother answered, I told her that she had to come with me now. She didn't understand. I made her.*~~

"Because you should feel guilty. You might as well have tied the straitjacket yourself."

~~*We got there. Your mother screamed. It looked like Jack was doing*~~

~~*something wrong. He'd tackled you. He was pinning you down. You were biting at him, screaming at him to get off.*~~

~~*But when you saw your mother, you stopped fighting. You stopped living. You gave up on all of us.*~~

Someone was grabbing me. Katie.

"Evan, stop it. Please, stop it."

And then I realized—I'd been screaming. The same scream. Your scream. That loud, inarticulate howl at the unfairness of the world.

It had stopped Dana. Stopped Jack.

~~*Dana, who had been there. Dana, your avenger.*~~

~~*I remembered your last words to me.*~~

~~*"So it's all come full circle."*~~

~~*I didn't know what you meant.*~~

~~*Only that, in your head, it made sense.*~~

~~*My response had been, "I love you so much."*~~

~~*But the circle had already closed.*~~

"I don't understand," I said.

"You destroyed her," Dana said. "You're the reason they took her away."

That was undeniable. But the question was whether it had been necessary.

It had been necessary.

I had to believe it had been necessary.

Betrayal or rescue?

Harm or help?

I was living in the space between the options. The uncertainty.

I looked at Dana. Which Ariel had she known? Which me did she think she knew?

~~*They packed you away. They told us we couldn't see you. They said you had to forget.*~~

~~*They wouldn't tell us where you were.*~~

"Have you seen her?" I whispered.

I could see: Dana wanted to lie. She wanted desperately to give me a convincing yes. But instead she shook her head.

Now it was Jack next to me. Jack putting his hand on my shoulder. Jack saying, "I'm sorry, Evan. I'm so sorry."

~~*Sorry. Sad. Mad. Sorry. Every day it's this cycle. Every hour it's this cycle. Sometimes every minute.*~~

~~*Don't you understand, Ariel? I knew the right answer, but I didn't feel it. I knew we were supposed to stop you, but I didn't feel it. Because it wasn't what you wanted. You wanted to die, and I wouldn't let you. The only thing I wouldn't let you do. And it felt selfish. Ridiculously selfish.*~~

Why couldn't you have felt like this? I had wanted to fall right into the earth, but now I was grabbing hold of the nearest person who cared. I was holding tight. I was finding strength in that.

And Jack. Jack held on, too. Jack was sorry, too.

Dana was starting to throw her things back in her bag.

"You'll always have Ariel on your conscience," she said. "Anything I did was just to make you feel her there. My birthday present. You have no idea how much I think about her. I can't go a minute without thinking about her. And what you did to her. If it weren't for you, she'd still be here now. She was drifting away from you. She was drifting toward me. I know that. And I know she wouldn't have wanted you to get away with it."

"No," Katie said. She reached down and took back the

photograph of Ariel. “You can’t speak for her any longer. Nobody can. That’s her job.”

“Give that back to me,” Dana demanded.

“You have to answer a simple question first.”

“What?”

“Did you want her dead? That’s the choice. Alive or dead.”

“It’s not that simple.”

“Oh, yes it is. Dead is dead. For whatever reason. And in a choice between life and death, there is no other choice. It’s life or death, period. These guys chose life. Are you saying you’d have chosen death?”

“I’m telling you, it’s not that simple. You’re ignoring what she wanted.”

“She wanted help. Not death.”

~~*You were always changing your mind. I wanted you to have the opportunity to change your mind.*~~

“She didn’t want help. She wanted freedom.”

~~*But death is not freedom. For a moment, it can look like freedom. But then it’s death.*~~

~~*Anything.*~~

~~*Something.*~~

~~*Nothing.*~~

I moved forward. ~~*It almost felt like you were with me now.*~~

“We did the right thing,” I told Dana. I needed to say it out loud. “We knew her. Yes, she wanted freedom from her pain. But she didn’t want to die. There’s a difference.”

~~*Now I saw you nodding. All the moments you were happy. All the things you wouldn’t have wanted to lose.*~~

~~*Maybe Dana loved you for your pain.*~~

~~*I loved you for everything.*~~

"What do you know?" Dana asked.

I shook my head.

"I know you can't hurt us anymore. I know it doesn't matter what you think. At least now I have more photos of her. Thank you for that. We don't need you to remind us of what happened, or when her birthday is. We remember just fine."

It was then that I felt you there. Not in the way you'd been that day—pleading, yelling, angry, full of doubt. But in the other way. The person I'd loved. I could feel you watching us, taking the snapshot of what we'd become. Four people in the woods, arguing over you. Clutching on to our versions. Yelling uncertainties. And I laughed, seeing it. Because I knew you would've laughed.

"What's so funny?" Jack asked.

"Look at us," I said. "Just look at us."

He didn't start laughing. Neither did Katie or Dana. But that was okay. It was fine if I was the only one who understood it.

23

After Dana was gone, Katie told us she knew where you were.

She'd written. You hadn't written back. But your parents had told her that you'd gotten the letters. That you'd read them. That you were doing better—some days more than others.

We all decided to write. I don't know what Katie said, or Jack. And I know it will be up to the doctors whether to share the letters or not. We talked to your parents about it. I had honestly been afraid that they would forbid us from doing it. I thought they blamed us. But it was pretty clear that they blamed themselves. It hadn't even occurred to them to blame us.

Dana still has her version. She will still hate us. But there isn't anything we can do about that.

I still have the photos, though. Even though they are as unreliable as memories. Even though I will only know my story behind them, not yours.

At least, not until you tell me yourself.

24

I miss you.

I love you.

I will never know every you.

I hope you're okay.

I used to think I would never see you again.
But now I think I will.

I'm glad you're alive.
I'm glad I'm alive, too.

I'm not sorry.

Acknowledgments

A Note from the Author

The idea for this book came, fittingly enough, from the photograph that is now on the cover of this book. I saw it stuck on the refrigerator at my good friend Jonathan Farmer's house and immediately knew I would draw Jonathan in on an idea I'd had: to do a photographic novel. Although I take photographs myself (at least one a day), I'd always wanted this idea to be a collaboration. And so it was.

Here's how it worked: Jonathan would give me a photo. I would write part of the novel, incorporating the photo. When I needed the next photo, Jonathan would hand it over. The whole book worked like that—photo after photo, one at a time. I never had any idea what photo would come next. And Jonathan had no idea what I was writing. He didn't read a single word until I was finished with the first draft.

I'd like to offer great thanks to Mr. Farmer; these words would not, in any way, exist without his photographs. Special thanks as well to: our magnificent editor, Nancy Hinkel, who makes my heart run round like a chicken with its head cut off; our fantastic designer, Melissa Greenberg, who rose to the challenge of this book; and everyone else at Random House, including the incomparable Jeremy Medina and Allison Wortche.

Many of my friends and family members heard about "the photo book" for years before it was finished, so I would like to thank them for their patience and support. In particular, I'd like to thank Jake Hamilton, whose photographs hang over my desk, and Zak Grimshaw, who was the book's earliest reader outside the editing circle.

The title comes from a Placebo song. Their music very much informed the writing of this book.

A Note from the Photographer

What a strange, wonderful journey these photographs have taken—from the remote forests of New Hampshire to the pages of this extraordinary book. My first thanks must go to Mr. Levithan himself, who, sharing my love of images, had the insane idea for this project, and who wove, out of my series of seemingly random images, a tale so exquisite I almost forget I had no clue what he was writing when I sent them. And to DJ Potter, my friend, collaborator, and muse, without whom these photographs would not have seen the light of day. I must also give thanks, for their friendship and support along the way, to Nadia Taalbi, Erik White, Brian Selznick, Danica Novgorodoff, Billy Merrell, Nico Medina, and the folks at Andy's Summer Playhouse. To my family—Mom, Dad, Seth, Katrina, and Jackson. And finally, to Ryan James Ouellette and Kate St. Cyr, my intrepid actors, thank you. Your faces captured my imagination; I hope this story captures yours.